Dear Reader,

Have you ever experienced the shock of discovering someone close to you has done something you'd have sworn blind they'd never do?

Jem and Eloise in my story have to deal with the fallout of just such a discovery. It's an emotional journey for both of them, but by the end of this book they've a new compassion for human frailty and an understanding of how small decisions can have big consequences. Of course, they've also fallen in love, which is always fun to write!

I don't know about you, but the idea of marrying into the landed gentry is a very beguiling idea. The United Kingdom is peppered with the kind of historic stately homes that would make any sensible girl drool.

Coldwaltham Abbey is entirely fictional, but the village of Coldwaltham is tucked away in the Sussex countryside. Nearby there's the medieval town of Petworth and its late seventeenth-century mansion of the same name. It was while I was walking in the 700 acres of deer park landscaped by "Capability" Brown that this story was born.

Now, if only Jem Norland had been walking the other way....

With love,

Natasha

"I'm sorry—" she began, but he interrupted swiftly.

"Don't."

It held her silent. She knew exactly what he meant. They'd come too far together for any apology to be necessary. He knew so much of her journey...because he'd walked it with her.

A deeply compassionate, empathetic man. From the very first he'd made her feel safe. He did that now. She felt safe. Protected. Loved.

Loved. The truth imploded in her head. Laurence's words echoed in her head, "a thousand small decisions" and then "as important as breathing."

ORDINARY GIRL, SOCIETY GROOM

Natasha Oakley

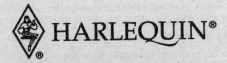

HARLEQUIN®

TORONTO • NEW YORK • LONDON
AMSTERDAM • PARIS • SYDNEY • HAMBURG
STOCKHOLM • ATHENS • TOKYO • MILAN • MADRID
PRAGUE • WARSAW • BUDAPEST • AUCKLAND

ISBN 0-373-03894-1

ORDINARY GIRL, SOCIETY GROOM

First North American Publication 2006.

Copyright © 2005 by Natasha Oakley.

This edition published by arrangement with Harlequin Books S.A.

® and TM are trademarks of the publisher. Trademarks indicated with ® are registered in the United States Patent and Trademark Office, the Canadian Trade Marks Office and in other countries.

www.eHarlequin.com

Printed in U.S.A.

NATASHA OAKLEY told everyone at her primary
school she wanted to be an author when she grew up.
Her plan was to stay at home and have her mom bring
her coffee at regular intervals—a drink she didn't like
then. The coffee addiction became reality and the love
of storytelling stayed with her. A professional actress,
Natasha began writing when her fifth child started to
sleep through the night. Born in London, she now lives
in Bedfordshire, England, with her husband and young
family. When not writing, or needed for "crowd control,"
she loves to escape to antique fairs and auctions.

Like Jem Norland in this book, Natasha owns a much-
loved pewter-colored Aga stove. She's a passionate
cook and all the recipes from this book are on
www.natashaoakley.com.

Books by Natasha Oakley:

HARLEQUIN ROMANCE®
3838—FOR OUR CHILDREN'S SAKE
3854—THE BUSINESS ARRANGEMENT
3878—A FAMILY TO BELONG TO

CHAPTER ONE

IT WAS true what people said—you were more alone in a crowd than any other place on earth. Eloise Lawton felt as lonely tonight as she ever had.

All she wanted to do was go home, run a bath and soak away her troubles. Instead she was here, making social small talk and avoiding the barbs of people who were fearful of what she might say about their dress sense. As well they might; she'd become more vitriolic of late. She couldn't seem to help it.

Eloise shifted her weight from one leg to the other, acutely aware of the way her Eduardo Munno sandals cut into the sides of her feet. Stunning to look at, but desperately uncomfortable when they were a size too small. Borrowed plumes for a woman who didn't fit in. Not with these people.

Everyone was vying for position, all judging the others on what they owned and who they were connected to. It was pitiful. Except it wasn't pity she felt. It was a deep, sickening sort of loathing. The kind that made her feel she needed to stand under the shower for half an hour to rid herself of the contamination.

But it was work. It paid the mortgage—and she didn't have the luxury of a handsome trust fund or an inherited ancestral pile. Unlike every second person here.

Eloise gave her wrist-watch a surreptitious glance and calculated how long she'd have to stick it out before she could make her excuses to Cassie. Not so long ago this kind of event would have filled her with excitement, but now…

Well, now things were different. A spontaneous decision to take her mother's belongings out of storage had changed everything.

It had seemed such a sensible thing to do. After six years it was certainly past time. She'd completed all the release paperwork without the slightest presentiment that she was opening a Pandora's box of emotions.

She'd known it was a mistake almost instantly. So many memories had rushed to crowd around her. Barely healed wounds had been ripped open and they felt as fresh and raw as when a lorry driver falling asleep at the wheel had altered everything.

She'd re-read the letter her mum had so carefully tucked inside her will and, six years on, she'd read it with a slightly different perspective.

Eloise let her eyes wander around the galleried grand hall. Enormous chandeliers hung down from the cavernous ceiling and huge displays of arum lilies, white orchids and tiny rosebuds had been tortured into works of art. No expense had been spared. Everything was perfectly beautiful.

A magical setting—but it felt like purgatory. How could it not? An ostentatious display of wealth for no apparent purpose. And her role in all this?

She no longer cared what colour anyone should be wearing or whether silk was the fabric of the season. When she sat at her keyboard tomorrow she'd summon up enough enthusiasm to get the article done but tonight it left her cold.

There was too much on her mind. Too much anger. Too much resentment.

'Mutton dressed as lamb,' Cassie hissed above the top of her champagne flute. 'Over there. At three o'clock.'

Eloise jerked to attention and swivelled round to look at the woman her boss was referring to in such disparaging terms.

'No, darling.' The editor of *Image* magazine tapped her arm. 'That's nine o'clock. I said three. Bernadette Ryland. By the alabaster pillar. Under that portrait of the hideously obese general.'

Obligingly, Eloise twisted the other way.

'In the yellow. Well, almost in the yellow. What was her stylist thinking of? The woman looks like some kind of strangulated chicken.'

Cassie wasn't kidding. It was a shame because the actress had been a strikingly beautiful woman before she'd succumbed to the lure of the surgeon's knife. It gave her face a perpetually surprised look. And that dress… It almost defied description. Certainly defied gravity.

Cassie took another sip of champagne. 'And Lady Amelia Monroe ought to rethink that haircut, don't you think? It makes her face look very jowly. Oh—' she broke off '—oh, my goodness… There's Jeremy Norland. And with Sophia Westbrooke. Now…that's the first interesting thing that's happened this evening. I wonder…'

'Jeremy Norland?' Eloise asked quickly, even as her eyes effortlessly fixed themselves on his tall, dark figure.

She'd seen a couple of photographs of him, one taken when he'd been playing polo and the other at a society wedding, but he was smoother-looking than she'd expected. Chocolate box handsome.

'By the door. Know him?'

'No.' Eloise's fingers closed convulsively round her

glass. 'I don't know him. I heard his name mentioned, that's all,' she managed, her voice a little flat.

'Haven't we all, darling?' Cassie Sinclair lifted one manicured hand and waved it at a lady in grey chiffon who'd been trying to attract her attention. 'That's the sister of the Duke of Odell,' she explained in a quiet undertone Eloise scarcely heard. 'Married a mere mister. Kept the title of Lady, of course, and makes sure everyone knows it.' She swung round to exchange her empty glass for a full one.

Eloise stood transfixed. Jeremy Norland. Here. Her mind didn't seem capable of processing any other thought.

Viscount Pulborough's stepson was here. In London. He was standing by the heavy oak door, his face alight with laughter. Not a care in the world.

But then why should he have? He was living a charmed life.

Cassie followed the line of her gaze. 'Gorgeous, isn't he? All that muscle's been honed by hours on horseback. And that suit is fabulous. Look at his bum in those trousers. The man's sexy...very sexy.'

'And doesn't he just know it?' Eloise returned dryly, watching the way he glinted down at Sophia Westbrooke.

'Can't blame the man for knowing the effect he has on women, darling. Looks. Money. Connections. Pretty lethal combination, I'd say.'

Eloise forced a smile. 'I thought he didn't like London.'

'He doesn't. He stays down in Sussex on his stepfather's estate. Makes tables, chairs, that kind of thing.'

'Fine cabinetry. Yes, I know.' Eloise sipped her own champagne. 'I read something about that.'

'You need a second mortgage to buy the leg of a footstool,' Cassie agreed. 'Sophia's dress too, I imagine. Do you know who made it?'

'Yusef Atta. Up-and-coming designer. Specialising in embroidery on chiffon,' Eloise answered automatically. 'Very romantic silhouettes. That kind of thing.'

'Worth a feature?'

'Perhaps,' Eloise agreed, watching the way the teenager gazed up adoringly. Sophia Westbrooke couldn't be older than nineteen. Could she? Whereas Jeremy was thirty-four. Thirty-five, perhaps—she couldn't quite remember from the Internet article she'd read two nights ago.

Cassie seemed in tune with her thoughts. 'Just back from Switzerland. Not a day over nineteen. And with a man like Jem Norland. Lucky cow.'

'There's no luck about it. It's all part of the in-breeding programme. Like marries like, don't you know?' she said in her best parody of an up-market accent.

Cassie gave a delighted chuckle, her acrylic-tipped nails clinking against her champagne flute. 'Wicked child. Now circulate, darling. Get me the gossip and no more ogling the natives. They bite.'

How true. It was a pity no one had mentioned that to her mother twenty-eight years ago when she'd first started work at Coldwaltham Abbey, not much older than Sophia Westbrooke—but Eloise would lay money on their fates being completely different.

Eloise watched her boss network her way back through the crowded room. Cassie didn't fit in any more than she did, but you'd never know it from her demeanour. She just owned the space, dared anyone to reject her.

Eloise had used to be like that, ambitious to the core—but things had changed in the past fourteen weeks. Fourteen weeks and three days, to be precise. The day she'd brought home those two crates. Who would ever have thought such a short space of time could make such an incalculable difference? Her eyes flicked back to Jeremy Norland, universally known as Jem.

He was the epitome of upper class living. His suit was fabulous. Hand-stitched, no doubt. Criminally expensive.

Money and opportunity had been poured on him from the hour of his birth. He'd the bone-deep confidence of a man who'd been to the best schools and who knew the old boy network would support him in comfort till the day he died.

And she resented him with a vehemence that surprised even her.

He reached across to kiss the cheek of the effervescent Sophia, who giggled appreciatively. He was so arrogant—it shone from the top of his dark expensively cut hair right down to his handmade Italian leather shoes. He knew exactly what he was doing—and the effect he was having on his youthful companion. Eloise just longed for her to rear up and tell him to get lost.

It didn't happen, though. Sophia smiled coquettishly and rested a hand on his shoulder. Eloise couldn't honestly blame her. She wasn't to know. It was years of sitting in a ringside seat seeing someone else's unhappiness that meant she would never be so stupid as to fall for a man like Jem Norland.

Anger and hatred had been building up inside her ever since she'd re-read her mother's letter and now she couldn't bear to be near these self-absorbed people who'd destroyed her mother's life so completely.

Her life.

With their grand houses, their horses and their public school accents. She hated them all.

A few short weeks ago she'd been fascinated by them. A detached and slightly amused observer. But now...

Now she had nothing but contempt for them.

For Jem Norland. The privileged stepson of the man she really loathed—Laurence Alexander Milton, Viscount Pulborough.

Her father.

Father!

That was a joke. He'd been no more than the sperm donor.

Six years ago, when she'd first read that letter, she'd been too numbed by shock to really take it all in. The sudden loss of her mum had been trauma enough and she almost hadn't had the emotional space to register what she now knew to be the identity of the man whose gene pool she shared.

Viscount Pulborough wasn't part of her life. He'd meant less than nothing to her. It was her mum missing her graduation ceremony that had filled her mind and twisted the screw of pain a little tighter.

So she'd packed all her mum's things away and scarcely thought about it...for six years.

Six years. Time had passed so fast. Life had been busy. There'd been so much to do—building her career, saving for her deposit, trying to pretend she didn't feel so incredibly alone in a big, frightening world.

There'd always been plenty of excuses as to why her mum's belongings should stay safely locked away. She'd had a small bedsit... She'd be moving on soon, so what was the point...?

The excuses stopped when she'd bought her flat. Her own home. It was time to finally sort out the last of her mum's possessions. All those things she'd put in box files and refused to think about.

The letter.

It had always been there. A time bomb ticking away—only she hadn't realised it.

Re-reading her mum's words six years later, she had found her emotions were different. She had a new, fresh perspective and, as she read, her antipathy had turned to anger.

It had been so easy to imagine what had happened that summer. Young, naïve, desperately in love, her mother had been swept up into a beautiful fairy tale—except for the fact that her prince had turned out to be married. More frog than prince. There'd even been a castle…of a kind. A brief spell of happiness and…what?

The rest of her short life alone. Struggling to bring up her daughter by herself. Crying over bills and juggling two badly paid jobs to make ends meet. A few hours' pleasure in exchange for a lifetime of pain and responsibility.

And did the esteemed Viscount ever think of that when he strolled about his great estate in Sussex? Did he?

All of a sudden she'd had to know. It had still taken weeks of soul-searching before she'd finally built up the courage to confront the man who had so bitterly betrayed her mum. And her.

And for what?

Nothing.

Eloise turned swiftly on her borrowed designer heels and walked over to stand by the open window. The buzz of traffic in the distance competed with the elegant strains of Beethoven.

A faint pulsing had started in her right temple and was shooting arrows of pain around her eye socket. She wanted to cry out at the injustice of it all. The total unfairness.

Jem Norland watched her, his eyes distracted by the flash of purple silk.

'Jem, are you listening to me?' Sophia asked, pulling on his arm. 'I'm going with Andrew to find somewhere to sit down.'

'Who's the blonde?' Jem cut straight to the question that interested him most.

Lord Andrew Harlington squinted across the room. 'In the purple? With the legs?'

'That's it.'

He concentrated. 'No idea,' he said, wrapping an arm around Sophia's waist. 'How about you, Sophy? Recognise her?'

'That's Eloise...' his girlfriend searched the deepest recesses of her mind '...you know, that woman off the television. Eloise...Leyton. No, Lawton. That's it. Eloise Lawton. The woman who does the clothes thing.'

Jem stilled. 'What?'

'She does that programme about style,' Sophia volunteered. 'Colours and so forth. Blue tones and red tones. It makes a difference to how great you look. She's really good at it. Writes for *Image* as well.'

'I'd heard that,' Jem said dryly, looking more closely at the woman who'd just pitched a missile into the midst of his family.

A blonde? Somehow he hadn't expected a blonde. Eloise Lawton—astringent, witty commentator on the fashion foibles of her contemporaries. This he knew. His mother and stepsister had told him.

But he hadn't expected the kind of cool, classy-looking blonde who might have stepped straight out of an Alfred Hitchcock movie.

'Champagne, sir.'

Jem pulled his gaze away. 'Thank you,' he said, reaching out and accepting a flute. He knew his mother would have counselled caution, but the opportunity was irresistible.

What he really wanted to know was why. Why now? Why Laurence? His stepfather was the gentlest of men. A deeply religious man, honourable and good. It was unthinkable...

'She is pretty, isn't she?' Sophia said at his elbow. 'Not your type, though.'

Jem looked down at her impish face. 'What?'

'Eloise Lawton. Very pretty.'

'Yes,' he stated baldly.

In fact, Eloise Lawton was beautiful. Beautiful, manipulative and dangerous. It was difficult to believe that anyone wrapped up inside such an appealing package could be guilty of such cold-blooded cruelty.

How could anyone dream up such a scam? And at such a painful, difficult time. Did she need the publicity so badly that she couldn't see the hurt she'd cause?

Oblivious of their amused glances, Jem made his excuses and threaded his way across to where she stood. He wasn't sure what he was going to say—not until the moment she looked up at him.

He saw the recognition in the depths of her dark brown eyes. He should have expected that. Someone like Eloise Lawton would have done her homework very thoroughly.

She'd certainly timed her letter perfectly. She'd selected the exact moment when the elderly Viscount was at his most vulnerable and the family would do practically anything to protect him.

He would do anything to protect the man who'd turned his life around. His anger crystallised into a steely coldness.

'Jem Norland,' he said, holding out his hand.

He watched the way her hands fluttered against her evening bag, the way she tried to smile before it faltered pitifully.

Eloise Lawton wasn't what he'd expected at all. It suddenly occurred to him how tired she looked. There were dark smudges beneath her eyes and they held the kind of expression he'd hoped never to see again. Such hurt. Almost hopelessness.

Slowly she placed her champagne flute on a side table. 'Eloise Lawton,' she said, placing her own hand inside his. It felt cold. Small.

He let his fingers close about it, suppressing every desire to comfort her. Whatever the appearances to the contrary, Eloise Lawton was one tough cookie. She had an agenda which would hurt the people he loved.

He knew, because he'd seen it, that the space for the father's name on her birth certificate had been left blank. Whoever her father had been, it certainly wasn't Viscount Pulborough.

Which meant?

His jaw hardened. It meant she was chancing her arm. Looking for publicity. He knew the kind of woman she must be. An 'it' girl. Looking for fame, for fame's sake. Famous for doing nothing.

And, God help him, he knew enough about that type of woman. They'd been the blight on his early childhood. The siren call his father had never been able to resist.

It was only… She didn't seem like that. She had more class than he'd expected. A gentle dignity…

She tried to smile again. He watched it start and then falter. 'I write for *Image*.'

'So I gather,' he said, releasing her hand. Her eyes flicked nervously towards the door. 'My friend, Sophy, tells me you're an expert on how other women should dress.'

'N-no. Well, I write about fashion, if that's what she means. It's all about opinion, after all.'

It was a diplomatic answer. She was clever. He had to give her that. And beautiful. Undeniably. A cool, serene beauty.

And beneath that…there would be…what? Passion? Fire?

And avarice. This had to be all about money, didn't it? About building a career. Using. Stepping on anyone to reach your goal.

Her goal, he reminded himself. She'd selected a vulnerable, ill, elderly man and claimed to be his daughter. With what proof?

None.

But she'd reckoned without him.

Jem forced himself to appear relaxed. 'And television? Sophy mentioned you'd been on television.'

'A little. I was asked to make a programme about the BAFTAs and I've done the occasional slot on morning television.'

Her hands moved endlessly over her evening bag. It didn't take a genius to recognise how nervous she was. She had good reason.

Laurence had stalwartly believed in Jem when he'd done everything he could to prove him wrong. He'd maintained a faithful belief in his stepson's innate goodness—despite all appearances to the contrary. And Jem had every intention of returning the compliment.

Laurence was not the kind of man to walk away from his responsibilities, whatever the personal cost. His sense of right and wrong was ingrained in the fibre of his personality. He could no more have rejected a daughter than he could have walked away from Coldwaltham Abbey. Both were sacred trusts, never to be abandoned.

'Do you want to do more TV?' he asked blandly.

'No.'

'No?'

Her fingers moved nervously. She placed her evening bag on the narrow table and picked up her champagne flute. 'Not really. It was exciting. Interesting. But no, I don't think so. I only really do it because it helps the magazine.'

'*Image*?'

'Yes.' She sipped her champagne. 'And it raises my profile.'

'That's important?'

Her eyes moved nervously. 'Very. Having a name people recognise is starting to open all kinds of doors.'

'Really?'

'Who you know is more important in this business than what you know.'

And Laurence was to be a casualty of that meteoric rise to the top.

But why Laurence?

Why try to use a man whose life had been beyond reproach? Someone who other people could look up to. Why be so cruel?

To his wife? To his family?

The answers came easily. She probably had a novel sitting in her bottom drawer she wanted publishing. All she needed was a 'name', a little scandal hanging about her, something that would persuade the big publishing houses to take a chance on her.

She sickened him.

'I'd like to write about other things. I love fashion but...' She broke off. Her gaze darted out of the window.

'You want more?' he finished for her. Of course she did. A high maintenance blonde, dressed in designer clothes.

She looked back, responding to the edge in his voice. 'Is there something wrong with that?'

'It depends what you're prepared to do to achieve it.'

Eloise frowned. 'Of course.'

Her fingers moved nervously on her champagne flute. His face was unreadable but she sensed he didn't like her. Perhaps it was for no other reason than he despised her profession. Many people did. But, perhaps…

Eloise quickly gulped another mouthful of champagne, the excellent vintage completely wasted. It could have been pure vinegar and she probably wouldn't have noticed.

She shouldn't have come. If she'd known Jem Norland had been on the guest list, she wouldn't have. Or any other member of Viscount Pulborough's family, for that matter. When she met them she wanted to be prepared, and for it to happen in her time and on her terms.

This wasn't the way it was meant to be. She wasn't ready. Jem Norland's startling blue eyes continued to watch her.

Did he know? Or didn't he? Had his stepfather spoken to him? The questions thumped through her head with the rhythm of a heartbeat.

'I understand from my mother that you're acquainted with my stepfather.'

Eloise tightened her grip on her glass. She could feel perspiration beading on her forehead, her hands become clammy. Her mouth moved soundlessly.

He knew.

It was a sensation akin to jumping off a cliff, the wind

roaring in her ears as she sped towards a fate she had no control over.

'Viscount Pulborough?' he prompted, as the silence stretched out between them. 'My mother's second husband.'

'We...we've never met.'

His right eyebrow moved in an exaggerated expression of surprise. His eyes travelled the length of her body, assessing and critical.

It was years and years of training that made it possible for a man to deliver such a non-verbal put down. Generations of believing you were somehow superior to every other member of the human race.

She really hated that he could make her feel so small and so worthless. If anyone should have been cowering with shame, it should have been him. It was his mother's husband who had abandoned a teenage girl carrying his baby.

'Really? I must have misunderstood what she told me.'

'My mum knew him. Years ago. I wrote to Viscount Pulborough to tell him she'd died.' Eloise carefully put her glass down on the side table and picked up her evening bag. 'He hasn't replied.'

Three weeks and there'd been no reply. Nothing. She hadn't expected that. She hadn't expected her father to welcome her with open arms—but nothing. No response at all. It seemed incredible. And with each passing day she felt more resentful.

How could anyone do that? How could he have created a life and care so little about it?

From the time she'd been old enough to ask questions about who her father was, her mother had said he was a good man. A man who couldn't be with them, however much he wanted to be.

His identity had always been a secret. But some part of Eloise had clung to the knowledge that he was a 'good man'. He would have wanted her in his life…if only it had been possible. He would have loved her. Loved her mother. He was a 'good man'.

Childish nonsense. He was a man who'd had too much of everything. A man who clearly rated people as worthy of notice or not worthy. A man who'd left a young girl to deal with the consequences of their affair alone and unsupported. A man who'd completely deleted the knowledge that he'd fathered a baby girl.

Her.

'He's been unwell.'

'Unwell?' Her eyes flicked up to his. She would swear his voice had become more menacing, beneath the suave veneer.

'But perhaps you know that already? He's been in hospital,' Jem continued smoothly.

'No. No…I didn't…I didn't know.'

Why would she have known that? She felt somehow that he blamed her. But for what?

'He's undergone heart surgery. A quadruple bypass.'

'Oh.' Eloise didn't know what to say. Considering Viscount Pulborough was a man she didn't know, had never met, it was strange to feel such an overwhelming reaction to the news of his operation.

'But at seventy-three it's taken its toll.'

She knew a moment of panic. He couldn't die. Not now. If he did she would never have the chance to speak to him. Would never know why he'd abandoned them.

'Could he die?' she asked, taking an involuntary step forward.

Jem held his ground. 'He had a stem cell bleed four years ago which made the procedure more risky than usual, but he came through the operation with only a small scare.'

'Scare?'

'His blood pressure shot up as he was coming round from the anaesthetic and they had to bring him round more slowly than they'd hoped. But he's making excellent progress now.'

'Th-that's good.'

'Yes, it is. The entire family has rallied round to support him.'

Eloise looked away, embarrassed. 'Of course. I'm sure... I...' She closed her eyes for a moment.

'Part of that is keeping him free of stress and making sure nothing's allowed to upset him.'

His words pooled in the silence. There was no possible way she could misconstrue what he was saying. From somewhere deep within her Eloise pulled out a quiet, 'I see.' And then, because she couldn't help it, 'You're protecting him from me. He hasn't seen my letter. Has he?'

'No.'

No. No apology, just an unequivocal 'no'. All these days, waiting for an answer that hadn't come. All the worry and nervous energy. The sick fear. The feeling of utter rejection. The anger.

And Viscount Pulborough didn't even know she'd written to him.

His precious 'new' family, his 'real' family, had closed ranks round him, lest he should be upset. Upset! It didn't occur to them to think how she might be feeling.

Of course it didn't. And if it had, they wouldn't have cared. She was beneath notice. An irritation. Someone born the wrong side of the blanket who was refusing to stay there.

And then there was a new thought. *Someone* had read

her letter. A feeling of coldness spread through her body. That someone had opened her letter. Read it. Dissected and discussed it.

It had been private. So difficult to write. She'd not imagined anyone reading the contents but her father.

She took a deep breath and met his eyes. 'Did you read it?'

'No.'

'Then who?'

'Does it matter?'

'They had no right to do it. It was a private letter. Personal. It doesn't concern anyone except...' She hesitated, uncertain how to refer to him. My father. She couldn't say that. The word 'father' stuck in her throat. 'Viscount Pulborough and myself. Not you, not anyone else.'

'Not even the Viscount's wife?'

Eloise met his critical gaze. 'No.'

She watched him check the retort he'd been about to make. A muscle pulsed at the side of his face. 'Why now?' he asked softly.

'Pardon?'

Jem smiled politely, his eyes flinty blue. 'I was wondering why now. Why make your claims now? Why not last year? Why this exact moment?'

Eloise drew a steadying breath. His words confused her. She didn't understand what he was trying to say, but she could hear the underlying criticism.

And then it hit her. Like a sledgehammer powering through the air, it hit her.

He didn't believe her.

The room around her felt hot, the air heavy with a mixture of cigarette smoke and perfume. Outside the open window the low hum of traffic and the occasional siren tore through the night sky.

Jem Norland didn't believe she was his stepfather's natural daughter. He was looking down his supercilious nose as though she was something he'd stepped in. It was none of his business, nothing to do with him but he dared…he dared…

She couldn't even begin to put words to what she was feeling. Her anger was incandescent. How dared he question her? Her mother? Did he think her mother hadn't known who'd fathered her baby?

He wanted to know why she'd made contact now. She'd tell him. She'd make him feel so small he'd want to crawl beneath the skirting board. 'Because I've only just realised how much it matters.'

She saw the frown snap across his forehead.

'When my mother died… There was a letter. Kept with her will.' Eloise found it difficult to speak. Her anger choked her and her grief was still raw. Even now. She couldn't do it. She couldn't go on.

Images of that day. The policewomen who'd come to tell her. The long drive back home. The shock and the emptiness. And the sense of disbelief as she'd read the words her mother had written in her distinctive italic hand. A letter from the grave. The truth. At last.

They'd been words her mum had hoped to say—one day. No dark premonition had made her put them down on paper. It was her usual, thoughtful care for the daughter she loved that had made her write it down and tuck it inside her will. Just in case.

At first Eloise had been too busy to think clearly. There'd been a funeral to arrange—and pay for. A home to empty. Her life had changed in a single second and she'd ached for things to return to the way they'd been before—even though she'd known they couldn't.

It was much later that the anger had set in. Six years later. When she'd collected her mother's meagre possessions from storage. A whole lifetime contained in two crates. When she'd really thought about the council-owned flat they'd called home. When she'd done that first Internet search and had seen a picture of Coldwaltham Abbey.

Her father had let them struggle with nothing. Nothing.

And then she'd re-read her mother's letter. Amazingly, there'd been no bitterness. Her mum had loved her father, had believed in him right up to the moment she'd tucked the letter inside her will. Probably until the day she'd died.

From that moment Eloise had felt a gnawing curiosity. That was *why now*. But how could a man like Jem Norland ever hope to understand even a tenth of what she was feeling? She wasn't entirely sure she understood it herself.

Eloise took a deep breath and tried again. 'My mother was involved in a head-on collision. Six years ago. A lorry…' Her voice faltered, tears blocking her throat. 'The driver fell asleep at the wheel. She d-died. Instantly.'

'I'm sorry.'

Eloise sensed Jem move towards her. She stepped back, her hand raised to shield her. 'It was a long time ago. You want to know why I waited until now?' She didn't wait for his answer, she continued relentlessly. 'She never told me who my father was. It was a secret. She told no one. She put a letter—'

'No one?'

The anger flickered back in her eyes. 'She must have

been a pushover for your stepfather. She just disappeared quietly. Went off to have her baby by herself. Never asked for anything. Never tried to make contact. Never…' Her voice broke on a sob. 'My mother was worth a million of him. It was his loss.'

CHAPTER TWO

SHE turned abruptly and pushed her way through the throng of silk and chiffon-clad women with their attendant dinner-jacketed swains, her heart pounding with an anger she'd never experienced before.

And sorrow. It had seeped into her bones. It permeated everything.

Her letter hadn't even reached the man her mother had loved. It had been passed around strangers. Her mother's secret had been shared with all the people she'd tried to keep it from.

Her own quiet, dignified request for answers, her need to understand what had happened, had been misconstrued. She felt violated and desperately hurt. Angry for herself—and for her mother.

Eloise found the ladies' cloakroom by pure instinct. She could hardly see for the tears burning behind her eyes. She pushed open the door and stepped down into the marble opulence.

Thankfully it was empty. She stumbled forward and let the tap run cold for a second or two before splashing her face.

He didn't believe her. She'd never expected that. She'd spent so much time imagining what kind of response her letter would receive. She'd never imagined for a single second it would be met with blatant disbelief and never reach the man she'd intended it for.

The door clicked open. Eloise glanced up at the two

middle-aged women who paused in their conversation the minute they saw her. She forced herself to stand straight and calmly turned off the cold tap. She didn't want their sympathy—or their questions.

As soon as they'd passed Eloise covered her eyes with her hand. She needed to go home. Decide what she was going to do now. Cry.

She needed to cry out the frustration and the anger. The sadness. The waste of it all.

Cassie wouldn't like it but she couldn't risk speaking to Jem Norland again. Why did he think her mother had lied? How dared he think that? She brushed away an angry tear.

The door at the end of the powder room clicked open. 'Are you feeling unwell?' one of ladies who'd passed earlier asked.

Eloise spun round. 'I'm fine. Sorry,' she answered briskly. 'I'm fine. Really.' She made a show of checking her make-up in the lighted mirrors and adjusted the narrow straps of her evening gown before leaving the ladies' room.

The babble of conversation immediately hit her as a wall of sound. The heat was stifling and the air was full of heavy perfume. Eloise pulled a tired hand across her forehead, easing out the tension, and crossed the room towards her employer.

'You look dreadful,' Cassie remarked as soon as she joined her.

Eloise let her breath out in a gentle, single stream. They were friends to a point, but Cassie wasn't the kind of woman you could confide in.

In fact, since her mother's death she'd discovered she really didn't have any friends she trusted in that way. Not for the things that were truly important, the things that touched your soul and defined your personality.

'It's nothing a good night's sleep won't cure,' she lied. 'I think I'll go home, though.'

Cassie's mouth thinned. She didn't like it. Eloise knew the signs of irritation well. Her employer ate and slept her job and expected everyone else to do the same. Nothing in Cassie's life was allowed to impinge on the really important business of running a magazine.

'Now?'

'I've got plenty of material.' Eloise glanced down at her watch and added, 'Which is more than can be said for Bernadette Ryland.'

Cassie's painted mouth relaxed into a half smile and she spun round to take another view of the actress's skimpy gown. 'True. But there are one or two people I'd still like to speak to, if I can.'

Failure wasn't in Cassie's vocabulary. She would speak to everyone she intended to—and stay until it was done. It was why she was as successful as she was.

Eloise followed Cassie's eyes as they searched out Monica Bennington, whose affair with a disgraced Member of Parliament had been headline news for the past week. A salacious story and Cassie wouldn't leave without some take on it.

'If you give me half an hour I'll come with you. We're all a bit jittery after Naomi's mugging.'

Naomi's recent attack had traumatised the entire office—but even that couldn't persuade Eloise to wait. Cassie's half an hour would become an hour, then maybe two. She had to leave now. Her temples had started to thud and she felt as if needles were being pushed into her eye sockets.

And she wanted to cry. Tough, sassy woman about town that she was—she wanted to cry like a baby. 'I don't want to rush you. I'll call a cab.'

Cassie's eyes flicked back to Monica. Eloise could see that she was torn as to what she should do. 'Alone? You're sure?'

'Positive. I'll be fine. It's not very late. I could even catch the tube but I'd look a bit daft dressed like this. Probably not the best idea for a fashion guru.'

Cassie laughed, as Eloise had intended she should. Her hard face softened slightly and she rested her hand lightly on Eloise's bare arm. 'Get them to call you a taxi from Reception. Bring the receipt in tomorrow. Keep safe.'

Eloise smiled her thanks and turned away. Thank God. Escape. Her eyes fixed on the double doors with the determination of a drowning man trying to reach shore. She'd never left an evening like this so early before. Had never felt such an overwhelming urge to run away.

But then she'd never met Jem Norland before.

The sudden cold blast of air was a relief. Eloise had never fainted in her life but she'd felt perilously close to it back in the ballroom. She took in a couple of steadying breaths, grateful for the comparative quiet.

Her fingers struggled with the stiff clasp on her evening bag before she managed to retrieve the small white ticket she needed to reclaim her wrap. With a nervous glance over her shoulder, she hurried down the wide-stepped staircase.

'Miss Lawton?'

She didn't need to turn round to recognise the voice of Jem Norland. Her fingers hesitated on the smooth mahogany banister rail and she stopped. 'Go away,' she managed. 'I don't want to speak to you.'

She carried on down the stairs, gathering up the fine silk of her skirt to keep it out of the way of her heels.

The marble-floored entrance hall was full of people and she had no choice but to take her place in a queue. He came to stand beside her. Tall and intimidating. 'I'm sorry.'

Eloise kept looking staunchly ahead. 'For what?'

'I've upset you.'

Bizarrely, he sounded genuine. Eloise couldn't quite understand that. He'd made a point of coming to speak to her when he'd known perfectly well who she was. He'd made it perfectly plain that he didn't believe her story. What exactly did he expect her to feel?

'I'm angry. Okay?' She turned to look at him. 'Not upset, angry. Very, very angry.'

'I'm sorry.' He kept his voice level and calm.

Eloise felt hot tears prick behind her eyes. 'Oh, go away.' Then, with a small break in her voice, 'Please, Leave me alone. Just go away.'

The queue moved forward and Eloise resolutely concentrated on handing over her ticket and reclaiming her wrap. She draped the soft folds about her shoulders, aware that Jem Norland had moved to stand near the reception desk.

Eloise looked back up the staircase to the oppressive portraits above. The sound of laughter and the general hum of conversation wafted down. She'd have been better off waiting for Cassie. If only he'd leave her alone.

She looked at the queue, which was five deep, all waiting patiently for the receptionist, and with sudden decisiveness she turned towards the exit.

Jem stopped her. 'We ought to talk.'

'About?' She pulled her wrap tightly about her shoulders. 'I've got nothing to say to you and I'm not interested in anything you've got to say to me. My mum was right when she decided to have nothing to do with my father.'

As exits went, it was pretty good. Head held high, she stepped out on the stone steps.

But it was dark.

And she'd meant to wait for a taxi. It was stupid to be walking about London at night, alone, in sandals with three-inch heels and wearing an expensive evening dress. She knew it.

But she couldn't go back. Stifling the panic she always felt about being alone at night, Eloise headed towards the main road. The street was deserted. Naomi had been unlucky. There was nothing to worry about, she told herself. This was a well-lit road in a good area and it would be easy to hail a taxi at Hyde Park Corner.

The wind whipped between the buildings and she pulled her deep purple wrap more closely about her shoulders as though it would offer protection. A shield against people who would do her wrong.

She pulled a wry smile. It wasn't even doing a particularly good job at keeping her warm. What was really needed on a night like this was thermal underwear and a duffel coat. Oh, and a pair of comfortable shoes. She'd kill for a pair of loafers right now.

A quick glance over her shoulder reassured her. There was no one. Not even Jem Norland. It was eerily quiet and, after the bright lights of Alburgh House, unpleasantly dark. It was strange how night made such a difference and made familiar places uncomfortable.

A sensible woman would have called for a cab from Reception; she wouldn't have let Jem Norland deflect her. She crossed the road and set out along the pavement at a brisk pace. Her skin seemed to prickle with an undisclosed danger. All the result of an overactive imagination, she chided herself immediately, but she still quickened her pace.

In the daylight this was a bustling affluent area. In the dark it seemed full of alleyways and litter. It was all fanciful nonsense, though, and the main road was only a short distance away. Lots of people. Lots of taxis. No problem, she muttered underneath her breath.

No problem at all. Keep walking, keep looking ahead, make it look like you know where you're going....

The wind picked up and Eloise sensed the first droplets of rain hanging in the air. Blast it. A drenching would really be a perfect ending to a miserable evening. She pulled her wrap tightly around her body.

It was getting colder and the wind stronger. Almost before she heard them she was aware of footsteps behind her. A sudden sound in the darkness. Her heart pounded uncomfortably against her ribcage and she quickened her pace, listening for the slightest sound behind her.

The footsteps seemed to keep pace with hers—although they were some way back. She took a deep breath to steady herself. She was jumping at shadows. A few more metres and she'd be on the main road. Plenty of people there, she reminded herself, but her heart continued to pound painfully against her chest.

With a furtive glance behind her to confirm there was someone coming up behind her, she saw a man still someway in the distance. Turning back, she did a few rapid calculations. How far from the main road was she? If she made a run for it, could he catch her? Probably. With her shoes off? Maybe not.

She let out another long slow breath. Time to discover whether not waiting in the Reception area had been one of the dumbest decisions she'd ever made. With a defiant toss of the head she crossed the road. And then she listened.

The footsteps stayed steady. For a moment Eloise allowed herself to relax. How stupid was she being? She was walking towards the main road; it was highly likely other people would decide to do the same. Then she noticed the footsteps behind her had quickened—and she heard the man cross the road.

Every nerve in her body was screaming as she resisted the overwhelming temptation to turn round and look. If she did that she'd be committed to flight and it wasn't much further. Not much further at all.

Eloise could see the corner approaching fast even as the footsteps sounded closer. The lights of the restaurants shone brightly. If this man got any closer she would kick off her heels and run for it. It was a question of timing.

Or she could turn and fight. Her mind struggled to remember what she'd learnt. Hand beneath the chin, knee in groin...

'Miss Lawton.'

She stopped and spun round to confront Jem Norland. Hot, molten anger rose even as relief flooded through her. 'Damn you. You stupid man! How dare you do this to me?'

Painful gulps of air shot into her lungs as she tried to control some of the anger bursting from her. 'Hasn't anyone ever told you that you shouldn't go following women, particularly at night, and even more particularly when they're on their own? It's an incredibly crass thing to do.'

'I didn't mean to frighten you,' Jem said, his footsteps slowing. 'I thought you'd seen me.'

'Just like you didn't mean to upset me? Why can't you leave me alone?' Eloise asked in a burst of anger before her chest contracted and she suddenly found she couldn't breathe. Her eyes opened in shock as she struggled to take in enough air, each shallow breath only serving to make her feel more frightened.

Jem took her face between his hands. 'Just breathe. In and out.' His blue eyes held her brown ones, the strength in them willing her to stay calm. 'It's okay. You're okay.'

Eloise didn't believe him but she kept looking up at him, the warmth from his hands giving her comfort. Her chest hurt and her breath was still coming in painful gasps. 'I'm sorry. I—'

'Don't try and speak,' he cut across her curtly. 'You're in shock. Just keep breathing steadily. In and out. If I had a paper bag I'd give you that to blow into.' He looked about him as though he might be able to conjure one up in the middle of a London street.

Eloise laughed, a hiccup and then a sob. 'I'm sorry.'

'What for? I'm the one that's frightened you. I should have called out earlier, made sure you knew I was there. I didn't think.'

As her breath steadied he let his hands fall down by his sides. There was silence for a moment as they looked at each other. Then Eloise shivered. Within seconds he'd slipped off his jacket and placed it around her shoulders.

'No. I can't—' she began but he stopped her.

'It's cold.' He looked up at the sky as the soft drops of rain continued to fall. 'And it's started to rain.'

He moved to place a hand in the small of her back and urged her towards the main road. After a few steps,

Eloise stopped. 'What are you doing? What do you want?'

'To talk to you,' he said, as though he were speaking to a child. 'We do need to talk.'

Eloise shook her head and her voice wavered. 'Why? You don't believe me.'

He put his hands in his pockets. 'But you believe it,' he said quietly.

His jacket hung heavy about her shoulders. She turned and walked towards the main road. He hadn't said he believed her, only that he believed she believed it.

And he wanted to talk. Why? But all at once she didn't really care. The most important thing was that she wasn't alone in a dark street. She hadn't been attacked. She was safe.

Still, after eight years, the memories of that night haunted her. She'd been one of the lucky ones, she'd got away unharmed, but in so many ways she was still a victim. Frightened of the dark, frightened of walking alone, frightened of being frightened.

Naomi's mugging had brought it all back. Had made that fear fresh. A large drop of rain fell on the fine wool of his jacket. Eloise glanced up and then across at Jem. 'You'll get wet.'

'I'll survive.' He gave a half smile and her stomach twisted in recognition of something. 'Where are we going?' he asked.

'To the main road. To hail a cab.'

'You could have got one from Reception.'

'I know.' She kept walking, her face turned away.

'But I was there,' he said slowly. 'Is that it?'

'Something like that.' She risked a glance across at

him. The rain had started in earnest and his crisp white shirt had begun to stick to his body.

It was a good body. Tautly muscled, as Cassie had noticed. She'd said he was sexy too, the tiny voice in her head reminded her.

And he was. Sexy. Strong. Safe.

Safe. Why had she thought that? Perhaps it was because of the way his eyes had held hers when she'd been panicked and fighting for breath. His hands had cradled her face.

Eloise looked down at her ruined sandals. 'I'll be fine now.'

'I'll find you a taxi.'

His voice brooked no argument and she was too relieved to protest. The lights of the main road ahead shone brightly, but she'd still prefer not to be alone. 'Thanks.'

'You're welcome. Having scared you witless, it's the least I can do.'

She looked up in time to see his blue eyes crinkling at the corners. Very sexy. But still the enemy.

He still thought she'd claimed to be Viscount Pulborough's daughter when she wasn't. What did he think she wanted? What could she possibly hope to gain?

'Why don't you believe me?' she asked suddenly.

Jem drew a deep breath and exhaled slowly. 'Laurence is a deeply religious man. He stayed married to his first wife for nearly thirty years, even when she was seriously ill with motor neurone disease. His opinions on the sanctity of marriage are very fixed.'

'So you think my mum was lying?'

'Laurence's name doesn't appear on your birth certificate—'

'How could it?' she responded swiftly. 'He didn't stay around that long.'

Jem turned towards her. His eyes were sad, compassionate, as though he didn't want to hurt her but believed he had no choice.

'I can't see Laurence ever turning his back on a child. It's out of character. He wouldn't do it.'

'But you didn't ask him. Did you?' Eloise hugged his jacket about her shoulders. 'You didn't show him my letter.'

'No. Not yet.' He stopped by the door of a lighted café. 'Do you want a coffee?'

Eloise glanced up and then through the window. The staff were clearing the tables. 'I want to go home. I'll be fine now, you go back to the gala.'

'I'm not going.' He slicked back his dark hair. 'I'm cold, drenched and I'm going to see you home.'

'What about Sophia Westbrooke? Won't she be looking for you?'

'Sophy will go home with Andrew.'

'Will she mind?'

'Why would she? They know I hate these kinds of events. I don't really like London. Too noisy. Too many people.'

They turned the final corner and stood beneath a street light, the rain glinting as it was illuminated in the soft beam.

'I'd read that.'

He glanced across at her. 'What else did you read?'

Eloise let her eyes scan the distance. She took a shallow breath. 'Your father is the late Rupert Norland. He died in a speedboat accident when you were fourteen and your mother married Viscount Pulborough eighteen months later. You were expelled from school. You design furniture and you're not married.'

'That's all?'

She glanced across at him. His hands were nonchalantly in his trouser pockets, his face mildly interested. 'You've a half-brother called Alexander who's at Harrow and who will ultimately inherit Coldwaltham Abbey. Rumour has it you were all but engaged to Brigitte Coulthard, heiress to the Coulthard retail empire. Since then, nothing particularly serious.' She raised an eyebrow. 'Do you want any more? I'm good at research.'

'So I see. I've no secrets then,' he said dryly.

Eloise pulled his jacket closely about her shoulders. 'Have I?'

'No.' He gave a half smile. 'I'm pretty good at research myself.'

There was a silence before Jem lunged forward and hailed a passing black cab. As the driver swerved over, switching off his 'for hire' light, Jem turned back. 'Where to?'

'Hammersmith.'

He nodded and Eloise noticed the way the rain was now dripping down the back of his neck, his shirt sticking to his back. His jacket around her shoulders was sodden, the bottom of her fine silk dress hung in miserable folds and her shoes were ruined.

She didn't care. About that or about anything. A strange fatalism seemed to rest upon her. Jem seemed inclined to make decisions and she didn't have the energy to stop him.

Settling back in the deep seat of the taxi, she didn't even comment when he took the seat next to her. It seemed natural he should. She didn't ask where he was going or whether this was taking him out of his way.

What if he were right? What if Viscount Pulborough wasn't her father? It was a small chink of doubt which made her feel like she was betraying her mother. But he was so certain. So very certain.

She turned her head away and watched the raindrops bead and weave their way across the window. Beyond it was all a blur of night.

Would her mother have lied? Eloise couldn't believe that. Wouldn't.

'Where to, luv?' The taxi driver half turned his head to talk through the open window.

Eloise jumped. 'Second on the left. Number fifteen.' She glanced across at Jem. His face was hidden in darkness but she knew he was watching her. She shrugged out of his jacket. 'You'd better have this back,' she said, passing it to him. 'Thank you.'

He took the jacket and felt inside the inner pocket for his wallet as the taxi pulled up outside her home. Jem opened the door and helped her out on to the pavement.

Eloise stood foolishly and watched him walk round to pay the driver. The rain had stopped but the pavements were dark and the air smelt damp.

Jem came back to join her as the taxi pulled away. As she watched the tail-lights disappear she glanced up at him. 'You'll never get another taxi round here.'

He shrugged. 'Then I'll walk.'

'That's silly.' Eloise shivered, her thin wrap doing nothing to keep her warm.

'Perhaps, but I'll be happier if I know you're safe.'

She turned and fitted her front door key into the lock. 'Do you want to come in for a coffee? You could ring for a taxi.' The words were out of her mouth before she even knew what she'd said.

'Coffee would be good.'

In the 'guide to all single women living alone in London' this was another foolish thing to do. You didn't ask a man you'd met that evening back to your flat. But even though Jem Norland was many things she loathed, she wasn't frightened of him.

She wasn't even sure she loathed him any more. It had burned itself out. It was the situation she hated and someone to talk to, anyone, was better than no one.

The traditional nineteen-thirties front door opened into a small lobby. 'My flat is upstairs,' she said unnecessarily. 'The house was divided ten years ago.'

'How long have you lived here?'

'Six months. I was lucky to get it.'

Jem followed her up the staircase and waited while she unlocked the second door.

'The lounge is through there. You'd better go in,' she said curtly. 'I'm just going to get changed.'

Eloise walked straight towards her bedroom, shutting the door behind her. She stood resting her back against the cold woodwork.

What was she doing? There had been no need to ask him in for coffee. No need at all.

There was no need for him to have accepted either, she reminded herself. No reason why he should have bothered to see her home. If he were so certain her mother was lying there'd be no reason for him to want to talk to her.

Eloise pulled out some dry underwear, jeans and a pale pink jumper from her chest of drawers, kicking off her Eduardo Munno sandals as she did so.

She slipped the narrow straps off her shoulders and let the damp fabric of her dress pool on the floor. Her skin felt cold and her hair was wet. It was so tempting to curl up beneath her duvet. To shut her eyes and let the day's problems melt into sleep. To forget all about Jem Norland waiting in her lounge.

Waiting. She pulled on her jeans and pulled the soft angora jumper over her head. He must be frozen—but she hadn't got anything for him to wear. She made a detour and grabbed a towel.

Why was he here?

She didn't want to talk about her mother. Not if he was going to criticise her and question her honesty.

In many ways it would have been better if she'd just folded up the letter again and forgotten all about it. Or burnt it, maybe. She should have trusted her mum's judgement. There must have been very real reasons why she'd decided to disappear quietly. Why she'd never tried to make contact.

Or had she? Perhaps she'd tried over the years but the Viscount hadn't wanted to know.

She walked nervously into the lounge. 'I'm sorry. I didn't think. You must be cold. Wet.'

Jem stood with his back to her, gazing down at the road below. He turned to look at her. 'It's quiet here.'

Eloise hugged the towel against her body. 'Yes.'

She had to pull herself together. To jump-start her brain in to some kind of working order.

What was the matter with her? She'd always had an answer for everything. Could cope with anything life threw at her. Just tonight it all seemed to have deserted her. She felt like a walking zombie. Like someone who'd had all their fire sucked out of them.

She tried again. 'That's why I bought it. That and the fact I could afford it. Plus it's only a short walk from the tube.' Eloise stopped. Total drivel. She was speaking total drivel.

He smiled. His blue eyes glinted down at her. Almost, Eloise thought as she was caught in their glare, she could almost forget he was the enemy. He had an uncanny knack of making you feel special. It was a rare gift.

Hesitantly she held out the towel. 'I've brought you a towel.'

'Thank you. Probably better to just lay it out on your sofa. Save the fabric. If I can sit down?'

Eloise shook her head. 'That doesn't matter.' Then, as she realised what he'd said, 'I'm sorry. Please do. Sit, I mean.' She rubbed a tired hand across her eyes. 'I can get you another towel, if you like.' She moved towards the door.

His voice stopped her. 'I'm fine.'

'Something to drink? I'm making a coffee.'

'Coffee would be lovely.'

His voice was rich and warm. A cultured voice. Safe. She watched him lay out the towel across her small green sofa before sitting down. Eloise closed her eyes for a second and forced herself to walk out of the room.

He made her small living-room seem tiny. He made her feel tiny, small enough to put in his pocket. She wasn't used to that sort of feeling. Eloise rubbed at her cold arms and shivered. Jem Norland was still the enemy, firmly on the side of the man who'd betrayed her mother's trust.

She had to remember that.

But Viscount Pulborough was fortunate in having someone so strong in his corner. There was no one looking out for her. No one to put their arms about her to hug her. She'd been strong for so long. Sometimes she just wanted...

Comfort.

She just wanted someone to tell her it would be all right. She missed her mum with an ache that was physical. It had been just the two of them for so long. She had always been supportive, loving and protective. And now...

Now she was alone. She'd been alone for such a long time. Six years.

For six years she'd fought her own battles and dried her own tears. There'd been no one to share the happy, triumphant moments of her life. She felt as if she was standing facing the sea and the tide was about to bear down upon her, an unstoppable force, and she would be swept away by the power of it.

CHAPTER THREE

ELOISE switched on the kettle and crouched down to search for the cafetière. It was tucked at the back of a bottom cupboard behind two large mixing bowls.

She sniffed the contents of an open packet of ground coffee, hoping it was still fresh. It didn't matter. None of this mattered.

Nothing Jem Norland could say would change anything. Her mum hadn't lied. Viscount Pulborough was her father—whether he wanted to accept that or not.

She glanced about aimlessly for a tray. She had one somewhere. Then she saw it. High on the top of the kitchen cupboards.

As she reached up with her fingertips it balanced precariously on the edge before tipping over, bringing with it a couple of bun tins and a baking sheet. Eloise closed her eyes and braced herself for the resounding crash.

She opened one eye gingerly.

'What the—?' Jem walked into the kitchen and began to pick everything off the floor. 'Not your day, is it?'

'I was looking for a tray.'

He held it up. 'You found it. Where do you want everything else?'

Eloise grabbed the tins off him and shoved them into the oven. Her mother would have had a fit if she'd seen her do it. It had been one of her pet hates.

Her hands shook as she rested the tray on the melamine work top. Why had she remembered that now? She closed her eyes and breathed deeply. When she opened them she saw Jem was watching her.

'All right?'

'I've been better.' She pulled out a couple of mugs from the top cupboard. Then she turned to look at him. 'Are you drying off?'

He smiled, the lines at the edges of his eyes fanning outwards. 'Steaming slowly.'

Eloise found her mouth curving in response. *Strange.* Awkwardly she turned and reached for a couple of cream mugs. 'Sugar?'

'No. No milk either.' He leant against the doorframe. Relaxed. Watchful.

Eloise tipped the last of a carton of milk into a jug and placed it on the tray.

'Perhaps you'd better let me carry it.' He stepped forward and picked it up. She stood back and let him do it, unusually passive.

Jem looked across at her. She looked absurdly youthful. Her chic bob lacked the sophisticated glamour it had had earlier. In bare feet she didn't reach his shoulder. Considering the damage she could do to the people he loved, he felt curiously protective of her.

And what if she was telling the truth?

More than that—what if it was the truth? What if she really was Laurence's daughter? It would mean Laurence wasn't the man of high ideals and personal integrity he'd always thought him. It would be a crack on the pedestal of the man who had done so much to restore his belief in others.

He followed her into the small lounge and watched her turn on the gas fire. The flames flickered up. She stood watching them for a moment and then turned to settle herself in the armchair, a cushion on her lap.

Jem carefully put the tray down on the old wooden trunk she used as a coffee table. It was on the tip of his tongue to ask if he should be mother. And then he remembered—her mother was dead.

That was what this was all about. He no longer questioned that her mother had left her a letter stating that Viscount Pulborough was her father. What he had to question, because he knew the man, was whether Eloise Lawton's mother had been lying.

And if she had been, the question was still why. Money was the obvious reason. Maybe it had been a clumsy attempt to provide security for her daughter.

Perhaps she'd even had an affair with the Viscount. Just two weeks ago he would have sworn it was impossible—but now...

It was possible. Maybe that was where the idea had come from.

But the idea that the Viscount would have turned his back on his child was unthinkable. No one who knew him would ever accept that as a possibility.

He was a man who placed huge importance on family. On duty and the care of others. It was what had persuaded his mother to take a chance on a second marriage.

And it had been a good marriage. His mother was settled and happy, a far cry from the woman he remembered from his early childhood.

Jem watched the way Eloise's hand nervously twitched at the tassel on her cushion, the burgundy threads stark against the pale blue of her jeans. 'Coffee?'

She jerked to life, every movement awkward. 'I'll do it. Sorry. I'm not thinking.' She cast the cushion aside. She pushed the plunger down and poured the dark liquid into his mug.

He pulled at the damp fabric of his shirt, then ran a

hand through his rapidly drying hair. This was crazy. He shouldn't be here. It certainly hadn't been his intention. He'd meant to warn her off, make it clear that Laurence wasn't alone.

Eloise poured milk into one of the mugs and gestured for him to pick up the other.

'Thank you.' He sat back on the sofa and watched her cradle her mug between two hands. She looked so tired. Beneath her eyes were dark shadows and there was a sorrow about her.

Not surprising, really. Life had obviously hit her hard. He sipped the liquid. 'Great coffee,' he said, a clumsy attempt to break the silence.

Her brown eyes briefly flitted up to meet his. 'Fair Trade. I buy it when I can. It guarantees the growers have received a fair price for their coffee beans.'

'I know.'

Her eyes flicked downwards. 'Yes. Sorry. I suppose you would.'

And then silence.

Jem had not felt so completely out of his depth for years. He'd forced this meeting. He'd followed her, frightened her. Had made the decision that it was something that had to be dealt with straight away... But now he was here he was reluctant to begin.

She was so fragile. Not the woman he'd imagined her to be. From her reputation on *Image* he'd expected to meet someone quite different. Not a broken butterfly.

He smiled and sipped his coffee. Butterfly was a good analogy for her. Particularly as she'd been earlier in the evening. Impossibly beautiful. Ethereal and fragile.

Jem glanced up. They had to begin somewhere and they might as well begin at the point of issue. 'When did your mother die?'

The hands on the mug moved convulsively. 'Six years ago.' Her voice was quiet. He had to concentrate to hear it. 'The twenty-eighth of November. I was away at university. They phoned.'

He didn't ask who 'they' were. He just watched her misery. Her body curved over her cream mug. Her face indescribably sad.

In the background was the sound of a clock, a steady ticking, marking the passing of time. And quiet. Jem set his mug down on the circular mat on the trunk, reluctant to break the silence. He watched the thoughts and memories pass over her beautiful face.

Because she was beautiful. The kind of woman men would happily have died for in centuries past. Had her mother been as beautiful? Had Laurence found himself irresistibly drawn to her?

'What was her name? Your mother?' he prompted. He knew the answer but he wanted her to talk to him. He wanted to understand what was going on.

'V-Vanessa. Vanessa Lawton.' She lifted a hand and wiped her eye.

Jem felt an overwhelming urge to walk across the room and hold her. The pale pink of her jumper, the soft texture of it. Everything conspired to make him feel protective.

Of course, she might be doing that deliberately, the logical side of his brain cautioned. But he couldn't believe it. Watching her, he had to accept that she believed Viscount Pulborough was her father.

And, moreover, that she believed he'd abandoned both her and her mother.

He shifted uncomfortably in his seat. 'How old was she?'

'Forty.'

Forty. No age at all. And then a new thought. Laurence was seventy-three. It would make an age difference of… He did a rapid calculation. An age difference of twenty-seven years.

Hell.

He frowned. 'Do you have your mother's letter?'

Eloise looked up, startled. 'Of course.' She stood up and placed her mug gently down on the tray.

He watched as she walked over to the bookcase and pulled down a plain box file. Opening it, she lifted the lever arch and picked out the top sheet. Wordlessly, she passed it across to him. 'It's her writing.'

Jem didn't doubt it. There was a quiet dignity about Eloise Lawton. Whatever was going on here, he was convinced it wasn't of her making. The sheet was closely written. He glanced up at her, suddenly unwilling to read her letter. 'May I?'

She gestured for him to continue. Jem lowered his eyes and read of a summer at Coldwaltham Abbey.

Every sentence, every paragraph, twisted the knife inside him a little deeper. He looked across at her. She sat back in her armchair, cradling her mug. 'This would make you twenty-eight?'

Eloise shook her head. 'Twenty-seven.'

Twenty-seven. He lowered his face to the sheet of paper and read on. All the descriptions of Coldwaltham Abbey, brief though they were, were accurate. And yet the records hadn't shown anyone called Vanessa Lawton working at the Abbey.

He wanted to say that, but one look at her face stopped him. Eloise had lost so much already. Carefully he folded her letter along the lines already there. 'Why do you think your mother refused to tell you earlier?'

She shrugged. 'Because he was married. I expect she was hurt by that, perhaps found it difficult to talk about.'

'And when his wife died?'

Eloise sagged visibly in her chair. 'I don't know.' Her hands clasped and unclasped the mug between her long fingers. Then she looked up. Her brown eyes were dark, soft like velvet. 'What's he like?'

Laurence? Like? Just a few hours earlier he wouldn't have hesitated to answer. He was a man of fearsome intelligence. Articulate. Loving. A great husband, father, stepfather…

Jem hesitated. How well did he know his stepfather? How well did one know anyone? You couldn't be privy to their every thought, feeling and action.

He placed the letter on the trunk, to the side of the tray. 'I'm sure he's everything you've read about him.'

His answer was pathetic. Eloise slumped back in her chair, obviously exhausted.

'Eloise…'

It was the first time he'd said her name. She glanced up.

'He's a good man.'

Something flickered in her eyes. He didn't understand it. Almost relief, as though what he'd said had given her immeasurable comfort. 'Will you trust this letter to me?'

Eloise shook her head. 'No.'

It was no more than he should have expected. The letter would have helped, but…

He couldn't blame her.

'I can't.'

'It doesn't matter. I'll speak to him.'

He passed it across the table. 'It doesn't say why she left.'

Eloise placed the letter carefully back into the box file and flicked the lever down. 'No.'

'Did she say whether Laurence knew she was expecting a baby?'

'She never *said* anything. All I know is in that letter.'

'That's it?'

She nodded.

'Had she talked about Coldwaltham Abbey before? Mentioned Laurence in passing?'

Eloise shook her head again.

'That's odd.'

'Why?' Her brown eyes were clear and bright as she looked at him.

'Never to have talked about a place that obviously meant so much to her.'

'Viscount Pulborough obviously meant a lot to her. She had his baby,' Eloise retorted swiftly, 'but she didn't mention him either. Some things are too painful to talk about.'

She stood up abruptly and walked over to replace the box file on the shelf.

Jem sat back on the sofa, his mind trying to meld what he knew of Laurence and what Eloise so obviously believed.

It just didn't fit. The man he knew would never have abandoned his child, however much he may have regretted the affair that had brought it into life. So, assuming Vanessa Lawton and Laurence had been lovers...

'Is it possible your mother left Coldwaltham without Laurence knowing she was carrying his baby?'

'No.'

He looked up. 'Why "no"?'

'She wouldn't have done that. No one would. Every

father has a right to know. She wouldn't... I know she wouldn't...'

A tear welled up and rolled down her cheek. Almost at once, Eloise looked down, the soft blonde strands of her bob swinging about her face.

Pain and loneliness rippled out from her as though she were the epicentre. Jem felt as though someone had punched him.

For the first time he wanted to kiss her. *Heaven help him.* Her face was so soft. So beautiful. The fine bone structure, the long arch of her neck... The curves of her body beneath the soft angora of a baby-pink sweater.

She was lovely.

And she was hurting.

'Do you have a photograph of your mother?' he asked abruptly.

Her brown eyes looked up again. She nodded. 'Of my mother when she was young?'

'Yes.'

'I think so.'

'May I see it?'

She stood up and crossed to a cupboard to the right of the fireplace. 'I retrieved a couple of crates from storage a few weeks ago. I'm sure there was a box of her photographs. I haven't looked at them. I didn't—'

Feel able to do it, Jem finished silently.

'I've still got piles of paperwork to sort through. Mum kept every Christmas card, every letter...' She opened the cupboard and pulled out a large cardboard box. 'Photographs are in here. I think.'

Jem squatted down beside her, lifting out the first of the albums. He opened the cover and looked at a young Eloise. She must have been about five. Her front tooth was missing, her eyes keen and bright.

He shut it quickly. 'Earlier than this.'

Eloise opened the next one down in the pile. 'I don't think it will be in any of the albums. There are some loose photographs at the bottom. I imagine they're more likely to be there.'

As she spoke Jem lifted out the next three albums and found a collection of photographs that hadn't made it into an album. Some had elastic bands wrapped round them. Others had been tucked into envelopes and bore inscriptions like 'Margate, August bank holiday'. Some were loose at the bottom.

He picked one up. It showed a young girl, not unlike Eloise. Her fair hair was loose and blown back in the wind. Her seat was an old tree stump. What astounded him was the oak tree behind that.

Jem's hand stilled and he peered closer. He knew that oak tree very well. He'd climbed it a couple of thousand times. It was the oak tree on the South Lawn. Now open to the public, but back then, when this photograph had been taken, it had been private land. Which meant...

What?

That Eloise was telling the truth?

That her mother's letter told no lies? That Laurence...was Eloise's father?

His fingers moved across the image. 'Is this your mother?' A stupid question, but he had to be certain.

Eloise glanced across. 'I don't know where it was taken. Before I was born. She was never as thin afterwards.'

'It's at the Abbey.'

'Is it?'

He nodded curtly, hating to see the hope that lit her eyes. It proved nothing more than that Vanessa Lawton had visited the Abbey. Hardly conclusive proof of paternity.

But it was enough to mean he'd talk to Laurence, sooner rather than later.

'May I borrow it?'

'The photograph?'

Jem nodded. 'I'm going back to Sussex tomorrow. I'll show him your letter. This photograph.'

'Thank you.' Eloise put the albums back in the box. Then she glanced back at him. 'Do you believe me?'

There was a part of him that wanted to say he did. But to say he believed Eloise would mean he had to accept that his stepfather had lied. And Laurence never lied. It was a pivotal belief.

'Honestly?'

She nodded.

'I don't know.'

He sensed her turn away, saw the flash of blonde hair swing across her face. Without thinking, he raised his hand and held her steady. He looked into her brown eyes. 'I'll show him your letter.'

Eloise nodded, her lips trembling, every emotion showing in her deep brown eyes. It was all he could do not to pull her closer. He wanted so desperately to take her face between his hands and kiss away the pain.

Instead he smiled and stood up, holding the photograph in his hand. 'And the photograph. I'll be in touch when I've spoken to him.'

She nodded.

Jem picked up his jacket and shrugged himself into the wet sleeves, placing the photograph in the inside pocket.

And he'd speak to his mother.

And his stepsister. If Laurence was Eloise's father he

could only have become so when he was married to
Belinda's mother.

Hell! It was such a mess.

'Thank you.'

Jem looked back at her. She had precious little to thank
him for. 'Go to bed. You look exhausted.'

And then he wished he hadn't said that. He could
imagine her snuggled beneath her duvet, her blonde hair
ruffled. His eyes drifted to her lips—full and sensuous.

'I'll be in contact.'

'Yes.'

She'd stood up. Her jeans hugged her thighs, her arms
were wrapped about her body. He wanted to pull her
close, rest her head on his chest and hold her.

Who was he kidding? He wanted to do more than that.
He wanted to slowly undress her. He wanted to peel the
soft fluff that passed as her top and cradle her naked in
his arms. He wanted to drive that wounded, hurt expression from her eyes. He wanted...

So much—and yet it was impossible. This was the
woman who was threatening the foundations of his
mother's happiness.

Eloise followed him out of the room and down the
narrow staircase. His clothes were nearly dry now. He
didn't really notice.

'Thank you for the coffee.'

Eloise smiled. 'Thanks for the taxi.'

'You're welcome.'

If Vanessa had smiled like that it might have explained
it. Jem pulled up the collar of his jacket and remembered
he'd intended to call a taxi from Eloise's flat. There was
no going back now. He'd head towards the main road
and hope something would pass. If not, he was in for a
long walk.

CHAPTER FOUR

JEM took the bend too fast and pressed down on the accelerator for the long straight before he realised what he was doing.

Laurence's tired face would haunt him until the day he died. The open remorse. The shake of his hand as he'd held the photograph. He would never be able to erase the image.

There was no room for doubt. Eloise Lawton was exactly who she said she was—Viscount Pulborough's natural daughter. One glance at the elderly man's face had confirmed everything. If he'd denied it, Jem wouldn't have believed him.

And in that moment something had died. He'd wanted to believe Laurence invincible, free of all human frailty. At fifteen he'd desperately needed that and somehow it had carried on into adulthood. He'd believed him to be a man above all others.

Laurence had always been a man to be trusted. A man to look up to. A man completely unlike his own father. He'd so needed that.

He pulled the Land Rover into a lay-by and sat. The sky darkened and tinted to a rich, dark red. And it was quiet.

Blissfully quiet. A few moments' respite before he telephoned Eloise Lawton. To say what?

To say that her father had at last been shown her letter. That Viscount Pulborough would be delighted to meet the daughter he'd neglected to tell his family about?

What would he say?

Should he tell her that his own mother had cried? Or that Belinda, her half-sister, had left the house refusing to talk about it?

It was as though the whole foundation of his adult life was suddenly unstable and in desperate need of under-pinning.

Secrets and lies. He hated it. Hated the sense of dis-illusionment that permeated everything.

Jem glanced down at his watch and jumped out of the Land Rover, eager to be doing something. Anything. He leant against the fence and rested his foot on the lowest bar.

In the distance he could see the old oak tree on the South Lawn. Tall, seemingly permanent, its branches spread out majestically, darkly menacing against the pink of the evening sky.

Impossible not to think of Vanessa Lawton who'd sat beneath it. Her face laughing up at the camera. A moment in time captured perfectly.

Laurence was a liar and a cheat. Had Belinda's mother known? Had she looked down from her bedroom window and seen her husband with Vanessa Lawton? Had Belinda known? He pieced together the dates and slammed a fist against the hard wood of the fence.

Belinda would have been thirteen. Old enough to have sensed something. Perhaps that explained the difficult re-lationship she had with her father.

Reluctantly he turned and walked back to the Land Rover. Telephoning Eloise was an inescapable duty. He'd promised and there was no one else to do it.

Truth be told, he wanted it to be him. He wanted to hear her voice—and that scared him. Eloise had the power to rip his family apart. His mother's carefully re-built life.

Eloise arriving at Coldwaltham Abbey could only cause pain to the people he loved. But what would this mean to her? Vindication, certainly. She was right to have had faith in her mother, whereas he…

He switched on the engine and took the road back home.

Eloise felt sick. It was the same kind of feeling she'd had on the day she'd gone to look at the notice board to discover her A Level results.

That day it had been good news, her place at Cambridge University confirmed, but it didn't seem possible there'd be a happy outcome today.

It was all too late. Twenty-seven years too late. Questions rolled around her mind in a ceaseless flow, but they could all be summarised in the one word—why?

Today she would get an answer. Summoned to meet the man who'd abandoned her mother—and her. What would she feel when she looked at him? Anger? Pain? Regret?

Love?

She had no way of knowing. Nothing in her life had prepared her for this. How could it? But the opportunity to come face to face with the man who'd helped create her was not something she could turn away from. However painful, it had to be faced.

She'd see Jem Norland again too. The man who'd made this meeting happen because he'd done what he said he would.

She hadn't expected that of him. Not really. The morning after the charity evening she'd have sworn he wouldn't bother. But he'd telephoned. The door to her father had swung open.

Even so, she wasn't a fool. His voice had been clipped, even angry. It wasn't difficult to understand why. He'd been so adamant that Viscount Pulborough couldn't be her father. He'd been wrong. Her mother had been right.

Her feet scrunched on the gravel of the drive as she forced herself to walk towards Jem's home. An estate cottage, he'd called it. But it was hardly a cottage. You had to have been brought up with his kind of privileges to describe it like that.

It was a solidly built, detached red-brick house with an impossibly pretty white gable. Everyone else's fantasy home. It reminded her of the gingerbread house in one of her childhood books. A far cry from the council estate in Birmingham she'd called home.

Viscount Pulborough probably had no idea what he'd consigned the young Vanessa to. He'd probably not given it a thought.

The familiar sense of injustice that had smouldered inside her over the past few weeks flickered angrily. She wanted Viscount Pulborough to know what her mother's life had been like. Ill or not, he had to know how much pain he'd caused.

And when she was sure he understood just what he'd done, she'd walk away. In no time at all she'd be back in London and he could continue his life unhindered. It was what he'd chosen, after all.

It didn't matter if Jem Norland didn't like it. He was obviously very protective of his stepfather, but it wasn't anything to do with him. Viscount Pulborough wasn't even his father.

Smoothing down her suede jacket, she reached up to ring the bell. The dark blue door was opened almost immediately by a man in his mid to late fifties, dressed in a red checked shirt and holding a steaming mug of coffee.

She was about to apologise for being in the wrong place when he said, 'You'll be looking for Jem?'

'J-Jem. Yes. Y-yes I am.'

'He's over in the workshop.'

She must have looked confused because he winked and said, 'I'll take you over. He'll be pleased to see you, I'll be guessing.'

He took a swig of the dark liquid and placed it on the small table by the door. 'Bess. Come here, girl.'

Eloise watched, stunned, as a brown Labrador padded down the hall and nuzzled the hand he held down to her. 'Do you mind dogs?' he asked, obviously seeing something in her face.

'No,' she replied carefully. 'Just not very used to them.' She glanced down at her cream trousers. 'Does she jump up?'

'Not this old lady.' Carefully shutting the door behind him, he nodded up towards a narrow path. 'The workshop's up there. No more than a couple of steps.'

Eloise glanced down at her soft leather shoes and stoically followed.

'I'm Matt, by the way,' He turned with a smile. 'Work on the estate.'

'Eloise Lawton.' Her feet struggled to manage the soft mud. 'Do many people work on the estate?'

'A fair few. There's thirteen thousand acres here. And the Abbey, of course. Always something that needs fixing.'

Eloise tried to nod intelligently.

'I'm the Estate Carpenter. Came as an apprentice to Pete and took over when he retired. Good few years back now.' They rounded a corner and Matt shouted out, 'Jem, lad. You've got a visitor.'

Eloise felt her shoe slip on the soft mud and she reached out for Matt to steady herself. The lines on his face contracted and he said, 'You'll need to get yourself some sensible shoes or you'll come a cropper.'

It was on the tip of her tongue to defend herself. When she'd set out that morning she hadn't imagined she'd be traipsing up a country footpath.

'You're early,' Jem said, walking out of the brick-built workshop. He shaded his eyes against the winter sun.

He looked very different from when she'd last seen him. Gone was the expensive suit and in its place was a pair of worn jeans and a T-shirt that looked as if it had seen better days. The effect on her was instantaneous. It began in the pit of her stomach and spread outwards.

Gorgeous.

Sex on legs, as Cassie had described. And completely out of bounds. She remembered the feeling of his hands on her face, the intent look in his eyes.

He walked towards her. 'I wasn't expecting you until ten.'

'It's half past,' Eloise shot back, her nerves as taut as a violin bow.

Jem glanced down at his wrist-watch. 'Damn, is it?'

'I'll be off then,' Matt said, tossing Jem a set of keys. 'Some of us have work to do. I'll take Bess with me. She's itching for a romp.'

Jem nodded. 'Thanks.' Then he looked at Eloise. 'I'll just grab my jacket and shut this place up.' He held out his hands to show her a pair of dusty palms. 'Better wash my hands too.'

Eloise neatly side-stepped a muddy puddle. 'Are we walking up to the Abbey?' she asked, following him, trying to ignore the way his denim jeans fitted snugly over a muscular rear.

What was the matter with her? Jem Norland was a representative of everything she disliked. He was a bona fide member of the moneyed upper class. She objected to him on principle.

Didn't she?

'Too far. We'll take the Land Rover.' Jem led her into the workshop, where the air was heavy with the smell of wood and dust.

Eloise looked round curiously. 'Do you work from here?'

He shook his head. 'This is purely my personal space. Everything I make here, I keep for myself.' He reached out and stroked the top of the enormous circular table in the centre of his workshop.

Eloise watched his tanned fingers splay out against the smooth wood. His touch was like a caress. He would touch the woman he loved like that. She forced herself to look away, suddenly aware of the burning heat in her cheeks.

Why had she thought that?

Perhaps because her emotions were heightened, her nerves pulled tight? It was nothing.

It would have made it so much easier if there'd been someone in her life who'd have held her hand through all this.

But not Jem.

His strength was appealing. There was something about him that would make it very easy to trust him, rely on him. She watched him turn away and walk over to a small basin at the far end of the workshop.

Jem glanced back over his shoulder. 'How are you feeling?'

An impossible question to answer. Nervous. Sick. Sad. Bitter. 'I don't know.' She tried to smile. 'Bit scared.'

Jem nodded, as though it had been the answer he'd expected.

She watched the way his muscles moved beneath the fabric of his T-shirt.

She rushed in, 'Th-thank you for arranging this.'

'There's nothing to thank me for. I merely did what I said I would.' He reached across and dried his hands on the taupe-coloured towel.

'I didn't think you would.'

'No? Well, that doesn't surprise me.' He folded the towel carefully into a long strip and threaded it through the loop of the towel ring. Then he reached up for a heavy sweatshirt and pulled it over his head, the blue picking out exactly a fleck in his eyes.

Eloise swallowed. *Gorgeous.*

'I owe you an apology.'

'Why?'

Jem crossed back to her. Eloise waited, finding it suddenly difficult to breathe. He stopped a short distance from her. 'I didn't believe you.'

'No,' she managed, nervously moistening her dry lips. 'I know.'

He pulled a hand across the back of his neck. Laurence…'

Eloise watched the self-deprecating smile, the weary expression that passed across his face. It told her more than he could have known.

She was stepping into a family that didn't want her. Of course they didn't. She'd known that. From the beginning—it was just that she hadn't thought about it from their perspective.

How naïve. She'd only thought about how she was

feeling. Her anger. Her resentment. But other people were involved too.

Viscount Pulborough…Laurence…was loved. Perhaps she'd cruelly made public his deepest, most shameful secret. Maybe he'd feared this day. Maybe her mum had known that and had loved him enough to keep silent…

She didn't know. And she hadn't taken time to think.

'Laurence,' Jem began again, 'was cross we hadn't shown him your letter immediately. He said we'd no right to withhold information from him. He recognised your mother's photograph immediately.'

Eloise felt her throat tighten and a burning sensation begin at the back of her eyes. 'R-Really?'

Jem glanced down. 'He called her Nessa.'

'Grandma called her that too.' Her heart jumped at the use of her mum's childhood name. Eloise hated the way she was so desperate for every snippet of information. She didn't want to hang on to every word Jem uttered, so needy.

He continued as though he hadn't noticed. He walked round his circular table, his voice bland. 'We hadn't been able to find a Vanessa Lawton on any employment records connected with the Abbey. Had I told you that? When your letter first arrived we spent some time looking.'

'She was a secretary,' she said stiffly.

'He told me. She came to type up his notes for a book he was writing.'

Eloise swallowed hard. She wouldn't cry. Wouldn't.

Jem stepped closer, his voice a deep rumble. His face seemed softer.

'It meant her name wasn't on the Abbey records.'

'Oh.' Eloise bit down on her lip.

Jem reached out and pushed back her hair, his knuckles

grazing her cheek. Eloise didn't move. She stood pinned to the spot as effectively as if she'd been nailed there.

It was a gentle, comforting touch. Eloise would have given a lot to be able to curl into it, to have him hold her. Just for comfort.

Or not. She felt as if she was in one of those daft turn of the century toys. The one you tipped upside down to make a snowy scene. Everything about her was shifting. Like being in a blizzard, with no point of reference anywhere.

She'd always been so certain of everything. And now...

Now she was certain she knew nothing.

'I'm sorry,' he said softly. 'Truly.'

He let his hand fall to his side and Eloise felt the soft brush of her hair on her cheek as it fell back into place. She sensed he was about to move away.

'What did he say about me?' she blurted out.

'I think he'd rather speak for himself.'

Eloise swallowed; it was almost impossible. A hard knot had settled in the middle of her throat. She'd never been as scared as she felt at this moment. She was completely prepared for total rejection, braced for it even. But desperately hoping for...

What?

She wasn't even sure what she wanted.

Acceptance? Some sense that she was not a 'mistake'? Not an accident of fate and bitterly regretted.

And where did Jem fit into all this? She didn't know. Didn't know at all.

'He said,' Jem said slowly, as though he couldn't resist giving her something, 'Alexander Pope wrote a poem called *Eloise to Abelard*.'

Eloise frowned, trying to understand the connection. 'I

know. In 1717 or thereabouts. It's one of the few things he ever wrote about love. My mum had a copy of it. It was where she…' She trailed off. *Got my name.*

Like a searchlight suddenly picking out something it had been hunting for—she understood.

'Laurence wrote a book on English poetry. Eighteenth century English poets, to be precise. It's his passion.' Jem turned away, but not before she registered the message in his eyes. 'We'd better get up to the Abbey. He's wanting to talk to you.'

He reached up to a hook on the wall for a large bunch of keys. Strangely, having come so far, she felt reluctant to leave. She'd have been happy if Jem had announced Viscount Pulborough had changed his mind and she wasn't going to meet him after all. She could cope with everything so far, but at the Abbey…

She didn't know whether she was strong enough for that.

'Will you be there?'

'If you need me.'

Her stomach flipped at his words. If she needed him. Did he have any idea of the turmoil surging through her veins? The uncharacteristic uncertainty.

'Will I meet anyone else?'

'No.'

It was the answer she'd wanted, but as soon as she heard it she wanted to know why. Did Viscount Pulborough want her to stay hidden in the background? Was he ashamed of her?

Or of himself?

'My mother intends to keep out of the way. There's no one else staying at the Abbey at the moment.'

Not Alexander. The fourteen-year-old who would be her half-brother. Jem's half-brother, too.

She glanced up at him. Strange. She hadn't thought about that before. Jem Norland was no blood relation of hers—but they would have a link between them. A shared brother. A connection between them. Always.

'Alex is away at school.' He steered her out of the workshop. 'And Belinda lives with her husband just outside Chichester.'

Belinda. Her half-sister. She'd seen a photograph of her on the Internet. There'd been a couple of short paragraphs. Very little to discover.

To her shame, she hadn't considered what Belinda might feel to be confronted with a half-sister. A half-sister whose existence meant her mother had been cheated on. Lied to.

She knew that Belinda was forty, married to the Hon. Piers Atherton and had no children. She knew the facts. She hadn't thought about the emotions.

'That's probably better,' she said, stepping out of the workshop.

'Laurence thought so.'

'Belinda's not going to like me, is she?'

Jem squinted up at the low winter sun. 'No.'

The single word hung starkly in the air. No. Of course she wasn't. Eloise had only thought about Belinda in terms of how unfair it was that her half-sister had received the best of everything, whereas she'd...

Whereas she'd had a mother who'd loved her.

And Belinda's mother had been ill and had died. With uncomfortable clarity Eloise suddenly saw the bigger picture. She might not have had an education at one of the best public schools, opportunities to travel and play a musical instrument like Belinda. She hadn't learnt to ride or owned her own pony. But she'd never felt unloved.

Never.

Her mum had always made her feel special. Had been completely behind everything she'd ever wanted to do with all the energy and support she could give.

'Does Belinda know about me?'

'Laurence told her.'

He'd told her. She could only begin to imagine how difficult a conversation that must have been. For them both.

They crossed the small courtyard, Eloise skirting around the uneven surface and small puddles. 'Why do you call him Laurence?' she asked suddenly.

Jem opened the door of the green Land Rover. He let his fingers rest on the doorframe. 'Nothing else to call him. He's not my father.'

He walked round and climbed in the other side of the car. He shut the door and settled himself in his seat before turning to look at her. 'My mother married him when—'

'You were fifteen,' she finished for him. 'I know. I read that.'

His smiled twisted. 'Your research. I forgot.'

'I was curious.'

'Of course.'

He twisted the key in the ignition and Eloise watched the movement of his fingers. 'Did you mind when your mother wanted to marry him?'

Jem turned his head to look down at her, surprised.

'Fifteen's a difficult age,' she apologised. 'I just wondered.'

'Honestly? I was as jealous as hell. In the beginning.' He looked back at the road. His hands moved smoothly over the steering wheel. 'I was away at school and came home for the Christmas holidays to find I wasn't as important any more. I didn't like it.'

'I can imagine.'

He smiled, the grooves in the sides of his cheeks deepening. 'I made life as difficult as possible for a few months. Got myself expelled from school.'

'You like him now, though?'

There was a momentary pause before he answered. 'He's been more of a father to me than my own ever was. I'm grateful for that.'

Eloise longed to ask what he meant. There was a wintry edge to his voice she couldn't miss. She hurried to fill the silence without really understanding why she felt she had to.

'I didn't want my mum to marry either. I liked it being just the two of us.'

'Was there never anyone?'

Eloise shrugged. 'There might have been a couple of possibilities...but I probably stopped any chance she had.' There was a short silence. 'I'd change that now if I could.'

'Would you?'

She'd not thought about how lonely her mum must have been. 'It can't have been the way she'd planned her life to be.'

It was all too late now. Her mum was long dead. Eloise turned slowly away. She looked down at her fingers, which were clasped in her lap. They were long, pale even against the cream of her trousers.

She saw the single tear drop down on her hand, a bubble of moisture which rested against her skin.

'I'm sure she understood,' Jem said brusquely.

Eloise swiped at her eyes. 'I'm not sure she'd have understood why I'm doing this. Contacting my father. Now. After all this time. It's only going to cause pain, isn't it?'

He said nothing. His hands moved against the steering wheel and his eyes stayed on the road ahead.

She understood why. She didn't need him to tell her the effect the sudden arrival of a mystery daughter would have.

'It's not my fault though,' she felt the need to say. 'You have to blame your stepfather for that.'

'And your mother.' He glanced across. 'It takes two to have an affair.'

'She wasn't married.'

'But she knew he was,' he replied. 'Don't try and apportion blame. You can't know what went on between them.'

Eloise pushed the palms of her hands tightly together until her knuckles glowed white. 'I know she was twenty-seven years younger than him. She was nineteen. Just nineteen.'

The same age as your Sophia Westbrooke, she added silently, forcing that memory between them. This connection she felt to Jem Norland was an illusion. She knew nothing about him. Didn't want to, either.

She looked back up at him, challenging. 'Who do you think carries the most blame?'

'Meet Laurence,' he said quietly. 'Talk to him.'

The flicker of anger smouldered and died. It was sensible advice. So much depended on what Viscount Pulborough said.

Eloise turned to look out of the window. The Coldwaltham estate stretched out to either side. Mature trees covered the grassland and a herd of deer grazed nearby.

And this belonged to her father. Had her mum been completely overawed by it all? So much wealth. Was that why…?

'When did the deer come?' Eloise asked suddenly.

'They're not just deer. It's a herd of dark-coated fallow deer.' Jem dropped down to second gear. 'And they appear in the records from 1624.'

Coldwaltham Abbey loomed up ahead. The pale stone façade looked both magical and intimidating.

They approached a set of large iron gates and drove over the cattle grid. Immediately the gardens became more formal. The lawns stretched out like a thick velvet carpet.

And her father owned this. It angered her.

She'd have loved a garden. Her own swing. A slide, maybe. She'd so envied school friends who'd had some kind of garden, particularly Isla who'd had a wooden Wendy house.

She glanced across at Jem's profile. 'Did you play here?' she asked, wanting to find something to fan her resentment.

'Not here. The Abbey is open to the public most days during the summer. There's a small fenced off area near the staff quarters reserved for the family.'

She sat back in her seat. Strange to own all this and not have the use of it. It was another world.

And she was about to enter it. An interloper. Unwanted.

'And there are the tennis courts. The stables are behind that. We have seven horses, four of which are mine.'

'Of course, you play polo,' Eloise interjected in a quiet, dead voice. The sport of the wealthy, she reminded herself.

He turned his head briefly to look at her. 'Most weekends.'

Jem pulled the Land Rover to a stop in a small courtyard. 'Laurence has commandeered a handful of rooms on the ground floor. The stairs are too exhausting at the moment.'

She was thankful for his matter-of-fact tone. She couldn't have coped with anything else.

Coldwaltham Abbey looked cold and forbidding in the grey February light. The windows stared blankly down and the whole thing reminded her of a museum.

This wasn't a home. Perhaps the current incumbent was as cold and forbidding?

Jem held open the car door. 'Ready?'

'Yes,' she lied, stepping down on to the gravel. Eloise had never felt less ready. How did you do this? How did anyone do this?

Jem shut the door behind her. 'I'll take you through to Laurence.'

Eloise nodded. Her knees felt weak and her stomach was churning. It was pure discipline that enabled her to keep walking behind Jem. Everything conspired to make her feel more uncomfortable, more hopelessly out of her depth: the high ceilings, the ornate doorways, the sweeping staircase.

She followed blindly, aware only of the rising panic inside her. Her shoes clicked on the limestone floor, occasionally muffled by the rich-coloured rugs. Walls of cabinets filled with beautiful china were interspersed by paintings.

Jem stopped at the end of a long corridor. 'He's through here. I'll introduce you and leave you alone. Is that what you want?'

'Aren't you staying?' She wanted to tell him she needed him. He'd said he'd stay if she needed him.

He thrust his hands into his jeans pockets. 'It would probably be better if I didn't.'

'I suppose so.' Eloise felt bereft. She glanced down at her cream trousers. 'Do I look all right?'

The muscle in his cheek pulsed but he answered smoothly. 'You look lovely.' And then, 'Don't worry. You'll like him.' A small pause. 'He'll love you.'

He turned the heavy brass handle and pushed open the door. Eloise could scarcely breathe, let alone command her feet to move. Somehow, though, she found herself following Jem into the cavernous room.

The furniture was of heavy oak but the room had a lived in feel. Fresh flowers were arranged in a vase on an oval table, a cheerful summer yellow.

Jem pointed at the far door. 'Laurence is still confined to bed. The operation is a very painful one and he's found it difficult.'

She looked where he indicated but said nothing. He strode out in front of her and Eloise had no choice but to follow. Her sense of fear was so real she could almost taste it.

Jem glanced back at her and smiled encouragingly. Eloise met his eyes and tried to smile.

'Ready?'

She nodded. For a minute they stood frozen, but to Eloise it seemed longer. It was as though time had become elastic and it stretched out between them.

Slowly his hand moved. He reached out and he touched the side of her face, his thumb slowly moving across her lips.

'Good luck,' he said softly.

Eloise stood bemused. She couldn't work out what was happening. All her emotions were swirling together in a vortex of conflicting sensations.

She knew he wanted to kiss her. She could feel his eyes follow the movement of his thumb. His hand fell away suddenly, as though he'd suddenly realised what he was doing.

He turned away, leaving her feeling bereft. She'd wanted him to kiss her. The realisation spread through her with a sense of shame. How could she want that?

The image of Sophia Westbrooke laughing up at him came up and bit her. So young. So beautiful.

Jem pushed open the door. 'Laurence, I've brought Eloise Lawton to see you.'

Eloise stepped through into the second room, her view of the bed shielded by Jem's body. She felt an over-whelming sense of panic and then a cold calmness.

This was what she'd been waiting for.

As Jem moved to one side, she looked at the elderly man sitting up in the bed. The expression on his face took away all fear.

This was the man her mother had loved.

Her father.

She stepped forward with a stumbling step. His hair was white and the lines on his face had fallen in pleasant places. A good man, her mum had said.

Over the past few weeks she'd vilified this man in her imagination but now she was faced with the reality of him. His eyes seemed to imply he expected her anger.

The angry red wound of his bypass operation showed livid against the paleness of his skin in the V of his pyjama top.

Viscount Pulborough looked steadily at her and then spoke softly. 'Eloise?'

His voice was hesitant and broken. She resolutely fanned the flames of her bitterness but they'd really disappeared, washed away in the wave of emotion.

Her father.

She heard the sound of the door behind her click shut and knew Jem had left her alone.

CHAPTER FIVE

DAMN it! He'd nearly kissed her.

Jem sat down on the Chippendale chair and leant his head back against the wall.

He'd meant to be kind. To be supportive of both Eloise and Laurence. Most of all he'd wanted to help his mother. If he'd refused the job of taking Eloise to Laurence she'd have had to take it on.

But he'd nearly kissed her. That hadn't been in his plan. He'd forgotten how beautiful she was. Had forgotten the shape of her face and the elegant curve of her neck.

Had forgotten, too, the vulnerability in her eyes. The sadness.

Jem brushed his hands across his face in a futile attempt to erase the image of Eloise.

Damn it!

This was a complication he could do without. He didn't want to feel any kind of attraction for the woman who'd had such a devastating effect on his family. Surely after everything he'd seen about love and marriage his cynicism should be protection enough?

'Has she gone?'

Jem looked up sharply at the sound of Belinda's voice.

'Has she gone?' she repeated with a nod at the door. 'Have I missed her? The not so dumb blonde?'

'If you mean Eloise, she's with him now,' he said, standing up. 'What are you doing here? We agreed—'

'You agreed. I don't think I said anything at all.'

Belinda pulled her jacket more closely around her painfully thin body. 'I want to see what she's like. Whether she's worth all this fuss.'

Jem moved towards her, his forehead pulled into a deep frown. 'Belinda, this isn't a good idea. You know it isn't. This isn't the time.'

Two spots of bright red burnt on her cheeks and he could smell the odour of stale alcohol. She'd been drinking. Automatically he glanced down at his wrist-watch and registered how early in the day it still was.

Her habitual resentment bubbled up. 'He's not your father. Even though he likes to pretend you are. He's mine. And he cheated on my mother. Mine.'

Jem reached out and took hold of her claw-like hand. 'This isn't the way to do it. Your argument is with Laurence, not Eloise. Tell him how you feel—'

'But not now! Wait until he's stronger. I heard you.' She snatched her hand away. 'But she can see him whenever she wants. Ask all her bloody questions about her slutty mother.'

Jem saw her head flick round before he heard the door open. Everything slowed down as though it were an action replay, but he couldn't stop the inevitable.

He saw Eloise turn to him with a question in her wide brown eyes as Belinda strode forward, her movements agitated and jerky.

'So you're Nessa's daughter.' Her voice held all the contempt, the pent-up bitterness she must have held inside for years and had never spoken about. 'You look like her. Are you a slut like her?'

The ugly word echoed in the large hallway, stark and hateful.

Eloise's mouth moved with some kind of denial, but

there wasn't time. Belinda's hand swung back and then forwards in a venomous arc.

'Belinda!' Jem shot forward, but not soon enough to stop the resounding slap across Eloise's left cheek. He saw her recoil, one hand holding the burning cheek and the other raised to protect herself from any further blows. 'Stop it. It's enough.'

Belinda turned to look at him, her eyes showing all the hatred she felt inside. 'It's not enough! It's not nearly enough.' She pulled her hand away from the hold he had on it. 'If you think I'm going to stand by and let her take over my father you've got another think coming.'

She drew herself up to her full five feet five inches. 'Your mother was a cow and everyone knows you're no better. Out for everything you can get. A hanger-on.'

Jem moved so he stood between the two women. He glanced back at Eloise. She said nothing and stood as though she'd been immobilised. Shock, he registered. He turned back to face Belinda.

'That's enough! Go home.'

Belinda sneered, her pretty face marred beyond anything Jem had ever seen. 'So she's got her claws into you, has she? Better watch out. Her kind only want money and you've got plenty of that. Perhaps she'd like to do a kiss and tell in that trashy magazine she works for.'

Jem heard Eloise's startled intake of breath behind him but kept his eyes resolutely facing Belinda. 'Go home,' he repeated firmly.

'I'm going. I've said everything I came to say anyway.' She spun round and started back along the hallway, her shoes clicking on the hard floors.

Jem waited until she had disappeared around the corner before he turned. 'I'm sorry, I…'

But he didn't know what to say. He watched Eloise's body sag as she crumpled with emotion, the tears falling softly over her pale cheeks. And he felt helpless.

There was nothing he could say that would take away the pain of that confrontation. She couldn't have missed the hatred in Belinda's eyes.

Her half-sister. The thought hit him like a bolt.

'She hates me.' Her voice sounded bemused. Lost, like a little girl in an enormous department store.

'She's angry.' He stepped forward and wrapped his arms around her body. Dangerous, he knew—but what was the alternative? The fine soft strands of her hair brushed against his chin as he pulled her close. And then closer.

He let his hand move to cradle her head, his fingers entwined in the gold of her hair. Her whole body seemed to judder and radiated with misery.

And all he could do was hold her.

He felt her sobs rack her body, the acute misery—and some of it echoed inside him. He knew she was crying about more than unkind words from a woman she'd expected to resent her.

It surprised him how angry he felt towards Laurence. The man he'd always revered. It was the lie he'd been living that repulsed him so much. With a secret in his past like this how could he take the moral high ground—ever?

Gradually Eloise's sobs quietened and her body relaxed. Her hair still touched his face. The soft suede of her jacket rested beneath his fingers. Jem pulled back and pushed the swinging blonde hair back from her face. 'All right?'

Her eyes were rimmed red and the mark of Belinda's fingers still stained her cheek. It was a stupid question.

He knew it the minute it left his lips but he felt so helpless.

And he didn't like to feel like that. It reminded him of how it had felt to stand by his mother, hear her racking sobs and know he could do nothing to help her. No one could, until she made the decision to help herself.

Eloise hiccuped and pulled back awkwardly. 'I've got a tissue somewhere.' She began to search her pockets. 'I'm sorry.'

'About?'

She swiped at her eyes. 'Crying all over you. Do you need to go after Belinda? I assume that was Belinda?'

'That was Belinda,' he concurred, looking up the empty hallway as though she might reappear.

Eloise bunched the tissue up into a tight ball and put it in her jacket pocket. 'She swings a hefty slap.'

'So I saw.' And then, 'I'm sorry.'

She shrugged, keeping her face turned away. 'It wasn't your fault.'

Jem reached out and touched the red mark on her cheek with his fingertip. He could see three fingers clearly marked on her skin.

'Has she left a mark?'

'For the moment. It'll fade.'

Eloise stepped back as though she couldn't cope with his touch any longer. 'It's turning out to be an unexpected day.'

'Is it?'

He watched the thoughts pass across her face. 'Not really,' she admitted quietly. 'I knew it was going to be difficult.'

Together they turned to walk down the long corridor, Jem slightly behind. Neither spoke. Eloise's mind was presumably taken up with everything Laurence had told her, and his with wanting to know what that had been.

Her whole body was held stiffly, the fingers on her right hand clutching at the strap on her handbag.

'When do you have to be back in London?' he asked neutrally, breaking the silence.

She turned to look at him, her blonde hair swinging back. 'Tonight.' And then, 'I'm driving back this afternoon.'

Eloise looked away and out through the large arched windows down an elegant vista. The whole aspect looked bare and wintry.

'I wondered if you had friends in the area.'

'No.' Again, that painful silence. Eloise couldn't seem to formulate any thoughts, let along put them into words. Everything she'd believed had been turned on its head.

She'd wanted to hate Viscount Pulborough—and yet she'd found him to be warm and compassionate. Hatred was impossible.

'Will you visit Laurence again?' Jem asked, interrupting her thoughts.

Yesterday she'd have been certain of her reply, but now she wasn't sure what she wanted. 'I don't know.'

They stepped out into the courtyard and headed back towards the Land Rover. Jem held open the door for her to climb up. 'Don't let Belinda influence your decision.' He walked round and sat in the driver's seat. He turned to look at her. 'Belinda is Laurence's responsibility.'

Eloise nodded, but Belinda's angry face sat at the forefront of her mind. She couldn't blame Belinda but she would never be able to forget the look of loathing in the other woman's eyes. How could she?

'They have a...difficult relationship. Ever since I've known her they've been...'

'L-Laurence told me,' Eloise cut in, her voice hesitating over the unfamiliar name. 'He blames himself. Wonders if she knew about his relationship with my mother.'

'It's possible.'

'That's what Laurence thinks.' She looked down as she felt the tears well up behind her eyes. For the first time she found she was blaming her mum. Had she known how unhappy Belinda had been? How scared and alone?

Perhaps she'd been too young, too infatuated with her new love, to realise how much hurt she was causing. Having met her father she couldn't believe the blame was entirely on his side and her mum completely innocent— despite the age difference.

Perhaps the most noble thing she could do would be to stop this now. To let this first visit to Coldwaltham be her last.

'Would you like to stop for lunch somewhere?'

Eloise brushed at the stray tears on her face. 'Pardon?'

'Are you hungry?' Jem asked. 'It's gone one. We could stop for a pub lunch.'

Part of her wanted to accept. The thought of returning to her London flat wasn't appealing. If only there was someone she could speak to about everything that was happening in her life. She felt so lonely.

So very lonely.

'You're busy. I don't—'

He shrugged. 'I have to eat. The Cricketers do some great food.'

Eloise hesitated. 'Are you sure?'

'I'm sure.' He swung the Land Rover down a narrow lane. 'It's not more than a couple of minutes from here and worth the slight detour.'

Bare branches overhung the lane, almost meeting in

the middle. In summer it would be like a bower. Beautiful. Eloise let her eyes wander over the detail in the hedges even while her mind was questioning the wisdom of this.

But the alternative was a service station sandwich and too much time alone. Too much time to think.

'Did you like him?'

She didn't need to ask who he was talking about. 'Yes,' she answered quietly. 'I did. Very much.'

'And you're calling him Laurence now.'

'He asked me to.' Eloise turned her head and caught the edge of his smile.

His eyes remained on the road. She wasn't quite sure how he felt about her using his stepfather's name. Maybe he felt everything was moving too quickly.

Perhaps it was?

The Cricketers was a charming old English pub, the kind you found in faded sepia photographs of bygone days. The roof was a mass of different angles and the walls seemed to bow out, the architectural style a complete mish-mash of centuries.

Eloise stepped down from the Land Rover and sniffed the fresh air. It had been the right choice. There was space here. Beauty.

And there was Jem. She turned to look at him as he locked the door. Laurence had spoken so fondly of him, had hinted at the deep bond of affection between them. It made sense of his initial attitude to her.

'Ready?'

She turned and nodded.

'This way then,' he said, indicating the low doorway. 'You might need to duck your head. The lintel's very low.'

Eloise's eyes took a moment to adjust to the darkness. Light came from the small panes of glass in the tiny windows and from the open fire at the far end of the room.

'It's beautiful,' she remarked, walking towards the fireplace. Around the mantel were the almost obligatory horse brasses, shining as though they'd been lovingly polished very recently.

She made a show of warming her hands in front of the flames—but it was only for show. Something to do.

Jem came to stand behind her. 'What would you like to eat?' he asked, handing her a menu.

She took it and gave it a cursory glance. It was difficult to think of anything as mundane as food. 'I'll just have soup.'

'Anything to drink?'

'A coffee. Please,' she added as an afterthought.

She was grateful that Jem hadn't asked her any questions. She wasn't ready to talk and wouldn't have known how to answer them.

The fire was warm so she slipped off her jacket and folded it with meticulous care before sitting down on the curved seat by the bay window. In the hearth the logs spat more than crackled.

Her head felt fuzzy as though too much information was swimming about in her brain. And she wanted to sleep. The effect of tension, she supposed. It would be so easy to take to her bed and refuse to emerge until this was all over.

Except it wasn't going to be over. It was the rest of her life. *Who* she was.

'One coffee,' Jem said, placing a white cup and saucer in front of her. Then, reaching into his pocket, he pulled out a small wooden cube with a number on the side and placed it on the table. 'They'll bring our food over in a moment.'

Eloise made an effort to snap out of her languid mood. 'This is nice.'

His fingers curved around the tall beer glass but he said nothing. His blue eyes flicked up and he watched her face, as though he were reading her mind.

'D-do you often come here?' she said hurriedly, and then winced at the clichéd question.

'Occasionally.' His fingers moved on the glass and she found her eyes were drawn to the movement. 'There's a pretty garden at the back. In summer it's a nice place to sit after a hard day in the workshop.'

'I suppose so,' she answered blandly.

'And, of course, it's haunted.'

Eloise looked up. 'Is it?'

'So the story goes.' He lifted his pint glass and took another sip. 'In 1760 the barmaid, Sukey Williams, fell in love with a wealthy traveller.'

'Did he love her?'

'Sukey presumably thought so. At any rate, she became his mistress…much to the chagrin of the local youths. One night she received a letter purporting to be from her lover, asking her to meet him in the spinney.'

Eloise sat forward. 'Did she go?'

'Oh, yes.' He nodded. 'She went. No one knows exactly what happened in that spinney, but Sukey returned to the inn with a nasty gash on her head and died in her sleep. Ever since it's been said that Sukey walks at night, still waiting for her lover to return.'

She gave a short laugh. 'Do you believe all that?'

'Me? No.'

'Nice story, though.'

He smiled. 'You ought to get Laurence to tell you some of the tales he told me about the Abbey when I first arrived. I doubt they're all true but they make good listening.'

Her face shadowed. 'Perhaps.' She tore open the top of the demerara sugar and tipped the brown crystals into her coffee.

Jem was a nice man. Whatever way you looked at it, he was a man to admire. This couldn't be easy for him, but he was…incredible, really. When you considered what she was doing to the people he loved.

The hatred in Belinda's face had been shocking. All her earlier conjectures about how her half-sister would feel had paled into insignificance before the real thing. Her half-sister hated her.

And what about Laurence's wife? Jem's mother? How did she feel about her husband's illegitimate love-child suddenly appearing on the scene?

It would be better for everyone if she just went away…

But there was such a temptation to stay. There was so much more she wanted to know about her father.

'I particularly liked to hear about the Civil War,' Jem continued, unaware of her thoughts. 'I'm convinced Laurence made up story after story to satisfy my cravings for adventure and honour.'

He broke off as the waitress brought across their food. Eloise smiled her thanks before trying a spoonful of her leek and potato soup. It was comfortingly warm and deliciously seasoned.

'Good?'

'Fantastic. I think…' she broke off and let the flavours swirl about her mouth '…I think it's got soy sauce in it. It's lovely.'

'Richard Camford is a genius. He took over this place a couple of years back. A refugee from city life.'

'You really don't like London, do you?'

'Not much.' Jem cut into his beef and kidney pie. 'Pleasant enough to visit, but I've got no yen to live there. I'd rather come to a country pub like this than follow the pack to the next up-and-coming restaurant. I don't like the big society parties either.'

'Why?'

His strong mouth twisted as though it were some kind of private joke. 'Because I prefer to have more say over whom I spend my time with. London parties are full of people I'd be quite happy never to see again. They bore me.'

Eloise thought back to the sumptuous events she'd attended for *Image* magazine. True enough, there were the same people over and over again. Different dresses, different themes, different venues—but essentially the same.

'But surely the polo set is pretty much the same people over and over?'

Jem raised his glass and drank before placing it back down in the exact centre of the coaster. He looked up, his eyes a vibrant blue with a hint of mischief. 'True enough, but the horses are interesting.'

She found an answering smile. Somewhere in the past half an hour she'd relaxed; her body no longer felt stiff and unyielding. She took another scoop of soup.

Jem had made a point of talking about other things. Anything. The cold sense of panic and fear had started to recede. Even the memory of Belinda's slap had softened.

'You haven't asked me what Laurence said,' she observed, her spoon poised mid-air.

'You'll tell me if you want to.' Eloise threw him a sceptical glance and he added, 'And if you don't, Laurence will.'

'Will he?'

His mouth twisted into a smile. 'That's his habit.'

'It must be nice to have that kind of relationship with someone.' She hated the wistful edge she heard in her voice.

There was no one, absolutely no one, she could tell her secrets to. It had never really bothered her before, but now, with so much going on in her life, she found that it did.

'You're in the wrong line of work,' Jem observed.

Eloise looked up at him.

'A journalist,' he clarified.

She smiled. 'A fashion journalist. Quite different. I'm just the girl no one wants to be at a party with.'

'I doubt that.'

His words hung in the air and Eloise found it difficult to breathe. There was a pain in her chest. His voice had deepened; his eyes seemed to be resting on her lips and all she could think of was how it had felt when he'd touched her face.

She looked down hurriedly.

'How did you get into it?' Jem asked smoothly.

'Work experience. During my A Levels I managed to talk myself into a two-week placement at a small magazine. I made coffee, answered the telephone and shadowed the stylist.'

'Then Cambridge and a first in English Literature.'

'Then Cambridge,' she echoed. 'Your research is good.'

Jem smiled and Eloise pulled her eyes away. What was happening to her? Why was it happening to her?

She struggled to bring her mind back to what she was saying. 'After university I went to work on the magazine, again for no money. I worked in a bar four evenings a week to pay the rent.'

'You must have been determined.'

'Oh, I was. There was no way I was going to have a life like my mum…' She broke off.

Jem paused and then asked, 'Was it so hard?'

'Miserable.' Eloise felt tears well up behind her eyes. 'You can't know what it's like—'

'I know miserable,' he cut in. 'Miserable doesn't necessarily have anything to do with lack of money.'

Eloise looked up, stunned. The anger in his voice was such an abrupt change, his words so unexpected. 'I thought…I thought you loved living at Coldwaltham Abbey.'

'The Abbey became my sanctuary,' he said, spearing a piece of broccoli. 'But by the age of fifteen there can be a lot of damage already done.'

'I suppose.' Eloise frowned. By the age of fifteen she'd known what it was like to go without. She'd never been on an aeroplane, she'd not been able to go to France on the school visit, she'd not been able to play a musical instrument because her mum couldn't afford the lessons.

But Jem? What had he had to do without?

And then she remembered he'd been expelled from school. A disturbed child, perhaps? Traumatised by his father's death?

And Belinda? If she had known about her father's affair she'd have known what miserable was.

Eloise felt vaguely ashamed. It was easy to forget that other people had their burdens; everyone seemed to have their own secret sorrow.

'My mum went to work at Coldwaltham Abbey when she was nineteen.'

Jem kept his eyes focused on his meal. Eloise watched for some kind of reaction, some flicker of interest, but he kept his face turned away.

'Laurence says it was like a thunderbolt. Like two halves of a puzzle.' She picked up her coffee cup and wrapped her fingers round it. The warmth spread into her cold hands. 'His wife…' She choked on the words, tears starting in her eyes. 'I'm sorry… Damn, I'm not usually like this.'

She put down her cup with shaking hands and shielded her face.

Jem reached out and laid his hand over hers. Her fingers moved convulsively beneath his. He sat there in silence, waiting. There was nothing he could say. Nothing that would make this an easier story to tell.

'I'm sorry.' Eloise pulled her hand away and brushed at the tear streaks on her face. 'I always seem to be saying that to you.'

She seemed embarrassed. Her cool, elegant façade had snapped and he would never be able to feel the same about Eloise Lawton again. She was no longer the icy blonde he'd first thought her. She would always be a woman of emotion, of compassion…

'I don't know why I'm crying.'

Jem felt the smile as it tugged at his lips. He watched as she bravely fought for control.

She made one last brush across her eyes. 'He told me about his wife. Sylvia. About her illness.'

'They were married for twenty-nine years,' he stated baldly.

Eloise looked up, her brown eyes soft and hurting. It twisted something inside him. He'd imagined she'd be cold and hard, but watching her now he knew she understood every nuance of emotion.

He wanted to make it easier for her, but the facts were difficult to tell. Sylvia had died of motor neurone disease, a cruel way for anyone to die but particularly hateful for the charming, educated woman that had been Sylvia.

For a man like Laurence it would have been agonising to watch. Jem drained the last of his beer. 'It was a long illness.'

She nodded, her blonde hair swinging. 'Laurence told me. He said how much he'd loved her and how difficult he found watching her suffer. He said he didn't cope very well and tried to ignore what was happening. He spent long evenings in his library and consoled himself by buying in the best help money could buy.'

This part of the story wasn't new to him. Laurence himself had explained how much he regretted the way he'd managed Sylvia's last few months. But an affair?

And to send his child away? It was still unthinkable.

'My mum arrived that summer. He said she was very young...and very lovely. And kind...' she sniffed '...he said she was very kind.'

Her eyes became distant and she seemed to be remembering things from far away.

'And they began an affair?' Jem prompted as the silence stretched on.

'Eventually. Laurence says he'd never intended it to happen...or imagined my mum would feel anything for him. Nessa, he calls her.'

Jem watched the way her fingers twisted together, an outward manifestation of the turmoil inside. 'But she did?'

'Yes.' Eloise drew a shaky breath. 'He said a hundred small decisions led up to their love affair. He said it began with something as harmless as a cup of tea on the terrace and became something as important to him as breathing.'

Jem could almost hear his stepfather saying the words.

He'd said, many times, that big decisions were made up of many little ones. He'd said it was important to keep a guard on the small decisions so the big ones were right…honourable.

For the first time he wondered whether Laurence's philosophy on life had been born out of turmoil.

'How long were they lovers?' he asked.

'Not long. At least not physically lovers.' Her hands began to twist again. 'Laurence said he'd loved my mum from the first few days of her being here. He thought he'd be safe because she wouldn't be interested in an old man like him.'

'He was only forty-five.'

'And she was nineteen. He described her as fresh and lovely, like a May morning.'

Tears welled up once more in Eloise's eyes. One single bead rolled down her cheek, leaving a silvery trail. Jem reached forward and wiped it away, almost without thought.

It was a mistake. His cynicism wasn't doing a good job of protecting him from anything.

Eloise was like a May morning. At twenty-seven she had more poise, more maturity about her face than the photograph he'd seen of Vanessa Lawton—but the similarity was marked.

He heard the small catch of her breath. Jem could easily imagine how a man would fall for such a woman. He sat back in his chair and waited.

'They read poetry together. Talked. They drank whisky on the terrace—' Eloise smiled '—and he almost forgot he was married. That his wife was ill and dying. That everything about his life was bleak…'

She looked up, clearly asking for understanding—and, amazingly, he found he could give it. He'd have thought that impossible. Affairs to him were inexcusable. They meant lies and deceit. They were an act of ultimate selfishness.

And perhaps they were. But he couldn't ignore the feeling of empathy and compassion building inside him. A forgiveness.

'It changed when he kissed her.'

Those brown eyes looked across at him and he felt his own gaze move across the angular planes of her face, coming to rest on the soft fullness of her lips.

'Before that they hadn't felt guilty. He says it was the moment they had to decide to walk away. But they didn't make that choice. Not then. The thought of not being together was too painful.' Eloise smiled, hesitant and nervous. 'Is it very wrong of me to be glad he loved her? Even a little?'

Jem didn't feel qualified to answer. His instinct prompted him to answer that anything that made Eloise feel better was good, but…

But he had other images in his head too. He could picture Sylvia, trapped inside a body that was refusing to work. Scared and lonely.

And he could see his own mother, confused and hurting when his father was alive. So many lies. So many new starts and desperate disappointments.

It wasn't Laurence. With the rational part of his mind, he knew it wasn't Laurence—but it was all knotted up together and he wasn't ready to untangle it.

'He didn't know she was pregnant.' She said the words almost triumphantly. 'He didn't know about me.'

Jem felt an answering surge of euphoria. 'Why didn't she tell him?'

'I don't know. He says he wishes she had.' Eloise smiled sadly, soft pain colouring her eyes. 'I don't suppose that's true, though. What would he have done if he'd known? His wife was dying.'

Jem moved through the different options. Laurence would have found the moral dilemma impossible to solve. Whatever decision he'd made, it would have been imperfect. 'What happened to Vanessa?' he asked quietly.

'Mum went home. Had me.' She looked up as the waitress came to remove their plates.

'Would you like anything else?' Jem asked. 'Dessert? Another coffee?'

Eloise shook her head and glanced down at her watch. 'I ought to get back to London. I don't like driving in the dark.'

'That was beautiful, Penny. Thank you,' he said with a swift smile at the brunette before turning back to Eloise. 'Shall we go?'

She nodded again and picked up her suede jacket.

'I'll settle the bill and drive you back to your car.'

'I ought to give you some money…' She trailed off as he stared at her as though she'd spoken in Portuguese.

Perhaps not. Maybe there was an unspoken rule among the rich and famous that the person who had suggested the outing paid the bill. Or maybe the concept of equality hadn't reached the upper echelons of society.

Either way, she wasn't going to let it bother her. Soup and a coffee wasn't going to break the bank or her feminist principles.

She watched him flick open his soft leather wallet. Expensive. He owned these things without giving them a thought. Part of his life—always.

He would never really understand what it had been like to roll over the sleeve of your school jumper in an attempt to hide the darn on the elbow. The embarrassment of knowing you were wearing the cast-off coat from Alison McEwen at number fifteen.

But he was kind.

'Ready?' He turned back to her.

'Yes.' She led the way back through the low doorway, pulling her arms through the sleeves of her jacket as she walked.

'Did you live with your grandparents?'

Eloise turned and laughed, the sound emotional and brittle. 'My grandma thought it shaming to have an unmarried daughter having a baby. She told everyone her daughter had got a marvellous job away somewhere and sent mum to live with her cousin in Birmingham.'

'Did you tell Laurence that?'

It had been unavoidable. Laurence's questions about Nessa's fate had been unceasing—and the answers obviously painful.

'I've told him the truth. I can't change what happened.'

'No.' Jem shut the door of the Land Rover and walked slowly round to the driver's seat. 'How did he take it?'

He cried, Eloise answered silently. It had robbed her of her need for vengeance. There was nothing she could do or say that would inflict more pain on her biological father than he would place on himself.

She forced a smile. 'It wasn't all bad. I had one fantastic parent, who loved me very much. That's more than some.'

'And you stayed in Birmingham?'

'Mum could have gone back home if she'd had me adopted, but she refused.' Eloise kept her voice devoid of emotion. 'Grandma came to visit us but we never went to her.'

'Never?'

Eloise shook her head. 'She was embarrassed. It ruined the image she had of having a perfect family.'

Jem glanced across, his eyebrows drawn together. 'That's terrible.'

'Perhaps.' She shrugged. 'People can only do what they're capable of. Lots of people are paralysed by the thought of what other people are thinking of them.'

There was a short pause. 'Is she still alive?'

Eloise shook her head and looked away. She'd died peacefully a couple of years ago. No one had grieved over-much; she hadn't been the kind of woman who'd inspired much love.

But his words reminded her how alone she was. There was no one left in the world who was there for her. No one for whom her presence was important. Not really.

It made Laurence's parting words more poignant. More important.

They followed the lane round and turned into the small courtyard where her Astra was waiting.

Eloise reached down for the door handle and was out of the Land Rover before the engine had stopped humming. She pulled her jacket closely round her body and waited until he'd walked round to join her.

She shivered as the wind whipped through the break in the hedge. 'Thank you for waiting.'

Jem slammed the door of the Land Rover shut, his hands resting for a moment on the metal. 'You're welcome.' And then, suddenly, 'Are you coming back?'

'I don't know.'

He turned round slowly and looked at her, his blue eyes startling against the grey of the February sky.

Eloise looked down at her shoes. 'It's complicated. I've said I'll think about it.'

His shadow moved across her body and his hands

reached out to hold her arms. Even through the thickness of her suede jacket his touch jerked her eyes upwards.

'Come back,' he said softly.

And then he kissed her. Gently on the top of her head, almost like a benediction. Eloise felt the tears smart behind her eyes. She stepped back, her smile wavering.

'I…I'd better go.'

'Yes.' His hands were thrust deeply in his jeans pockets.

She lifted her hand in a small half-hearted wave before climbing into her car and driving away.

CHAPTER SIX

ELOISE glanced down at the softly swinging ivory skirt of her dress with a sense of guilt. Classically elegant and beautifully understated, it had cost a fortune. She would suit the environs of Coldwaltham Abbey perfectly, but it had cost more money than she had to spare.

And just who was she trying to impress? And why? She would like to have believed it was her father, but...

She couldn't fool herself. There would be other people to impress today. Her father's second wife, her half-brother, her half-sister...

Jem.

Jem. Eloise clutched at the small gift she held in her hand. She didn't like the way Jem Norland had started to fill her mind. It was inevitable she would think of him to some degree—he'd been so involved in her first meeting with her father, but...

Did she really have to behave like a nervous teenager whenever he phoned? Or wonder whether he was pleased she'd decided to accept a second invitation to the Abbey? She couldn't tell from his voice or from what he said. There was always the suspicion that he was charming simply because he couldn't be anything else.

As she headed for the central steps, she took a moment to steady her breathing. This time she'd have to walk in the main entrance. Alone.

It was so difficult. Walking into Coldwaltham Abbey alone was like removing your armour without knowing whether you were going to be killed. She'd always been so self-sufficient, so confident, but the potential for being hurt was immense.

Outwardly Eloise appeared calm, her habitual poise completely intact. Her hair hung in a smooth curtain, her make-up flawless, and the shape and colour of her dress a testament to her skill as a style guru.

She could do this. Of course she could. Her stomach churned unpleasantly as she forced herself to walk forwards. The main entrance to the Abbey was so imposing. So grand.

It had probably been a mistake to come. She wouldn't be wanted. How could she be? Countless times over the past few days she'd decided to make a telephone call to her father and cancel, but something had always held her back.

And here she was. A guest at her father's seventy-fourth birthday. A small, select gathering. Just the family.

The wide door swung open before she'd climbed the first of the steps.

'Hello,' she began foolishly, 'I—I'm Eloise Lawton.'

The butler smiled. It was professional perfection. Just the right mix of confidence, warmth and servility.

'The family are expecting you, Miss Lawton. They're in the Winter Sitting Room. If you'll follow me?'

Divested of her soft wool coat she followed, desperately conscious of the opulence and the intimidating formality. The entrance hall had been designed to impress and it entirely met all the expectations of that long-ago architect.

Eloise stepped through the doorway into the Winter Sitting Room, the butler's understated announcement ringing in her ears. Her fingers convulsively gripped the present and her smile was over-bright.

The immediate impression was of warmth. Along one

wall heavy curtains in a paisley pattern hung at the four floor-to-ceiling windows. Large sofas in a rich burgundy were arranged symmetrically around the open fireplace.

Then her eyes took in the people. Just the four of them, all turned towards her. Jem winked, almost imperceptibly, but Eloise noticed and her stomach fluttered.

It seemed such a long time ago she'd thought him just chocolate box handsome. Now his presence seemed to electrify the room. Resolutely she turned away, the mere knowledge he was there, watching her, supporting her, gave her strength.

The Viscount—her father—immediately came forward to greet her. He looked so much better than at their first meeting. His pleasantly lined face was smiling with genuine pleasure at her arrival.

'Eloise, my dear, I'm so glad you were able to come,' he said, drawing her into the centre of the room. 'It's ridiculous to celebrate birthdays at my age, but this year I felt I really had to.'

'Happy birthday,' she murmured. 'I brought you…a gift. I wasn't sure what you would like. It's only a token, I…' Eloise let the words trail off as she held out the oblong package tied up with deep burgundy ribbon.

This felt so strange. In her mind she played over the years when she hadn't had a father to buy presents for. Was he thinking of that?

The Viscount squeezed her hand as he took the parcel from her. 'I'm delighted you're here. Now,' he said, turning away, 'let me introduce you to my wife.'

He led Eloise towards a woman she recognised instantly as being Jem's mother. Standing side by side the similarity between the two was startling. Mostly it was because of the eyes, a startling blue, Eloise thought as she accepted the hand offered her.

'You must call me Marie,' she said with the faintest trace of a French accent. Eloise had forgotten that she'd read that. Somewhere in all her research there'd been mention that the Viscountess was French by birth.

'Marie,' she repeated obediently.

Marie stood gracefully and smiled. 'This must be very difficult for you, but you must know we are all delighted to have you to join us for Laurence's birthday.'

'Thank you.'

'My son, Jeremy, you already know.' Her voice with its husky accent gave his name a sexy uplift.

Eloise turned briefly and acknowledged him with a smile, unaccountably embarrassed. 'He's been very kind.'

'And this is Alexander. The son Laurence and I share together.' She indicated the one remaining person in the room, a coltishly handsome boy of about fourteen.

Her half-brother.

Eloise looked at him curiously, wanting to see some similarities between them. Alexander looked back at her with equal interest.

'How do you do?' he said with the unmistakeable accent of one of Britain's top public schools.

'Lovely to meet you,' she murmured.

His mother interrupted. 'Sit beside me, Eloise. That is such a beautiful name.'

'It's from a poem,' Eloise said carefully.

Marie smiled, a merry twinkle in the depths of her blue eyes. 'So I know. It was inspired by one of France's greatest love stories, but so tragic.' Her hands spread out expressively. 'Your mother shared Laurence's love of eighteenth century English poets?'

'I—I don't think so. Not really.'

The Viscount interrupted. 'You were born on the anniversary of Pope's birthday. Nessa would have known that.'

'The twenty-first of May?' Eloise turned to look at him.

'1688.' He nodded. 'Quite a remarkable coincidence.'

His wife smiled, turning back to Eloise. 'I'm so sorry I didn't show Laurence your letter immediately. If I had known of my husband's relationship with your mother, I would have done so.' She reached out and took hold of her hand. 'I hope you will be able to forgive me.'

Eloise cleared her throat. 'Of course.'

'I thought he had no secrets from me, but I have found him to be more…surprising than I thought,' she said, releasing her hand.

The Viscount moved to stand behind his wife and laid a gentle hand on her shoulder. Marie reached up and placed her own on top of it. 'Open your present, Laurence.'

Jem stood up and walked over to a circular table with cut-glass decanters on it. Eloise immediately glanced across at him.

'What would you like to drink?' he asked.

'Nothing. Thank you.'

'You're sure?'

Eloise nodded. She was too nervous to drink.

Jem poured out a small glass of sherry and handed it to his mother. He looked completely comfortable and at home in this environment—which, of course, he was. A world apart from the one she'd known.

What would it have been like to have grown up in a place like this? She felt a small dart of envy. For the first time in her life she understood what people meant when they talked about it being a privilege and a sacred trust.

The Viscount untied the ribbon and revealed a biography of Samuel Johnson. 'It's written by a friend of mine,' Eloise said, almost apologetically. 'We were at university together.'

'Cambridge,' Jem cut in. 'English Literature.'

The Viscount looked up, his eyes suspiciously moist. 'My own university.' And then, 'I see you share my passion for books. Dr Johnson was a remarkable man.'

'Wasn't he the man who wrote the *Dictionary of the English Language*?' Jem asked, strolling over to peer down at the book.

'1755,' his stepfather said, flicking his eyes over the bibliography. 'Brilliantly clever and very witty. I love his definition of angling as "a stick and a string with a worm on one end and a fool on the other".' He looked up at Jem's crack of laughter. 'Can't abide that sport. Total waste of time.'

'Have you seen a copy of Laurence's book?' Marie asked softly, watching Eloise's face.

'No.'

'Oh, Laurence,' she said, turning to her husband. 'You should have shown her.' She looked back at Eloise. 'Your father dedicated it to "Nessa". Your mother. *Oui*?'

Laurence shut the biography. 'I will fetch it from the library after lunch.'

'Jeremy—' Marie turned to her elder son '—why don't you show Eloise now? I'm sure she'd love to see it…and we are still waiting for Belinda and Piers.'

'No. Really,' Eloise began. 'It doesn't matter. I—'

Marie stopped her. 'Until very recently I had no idea who Nessa was.' She smiled at her husband and said softly, 'Or how important.'

She must have caught something of Eloise's surprise because she added, 'I see no point in pretending we do not know what we all know. It is quite ridiculous,' she said with a dismissive wave of her hand, 'particularly when Eloise is such a delightful addition to our family. Would you like to see the book, *petite*? It's the start of your story.'

Jem stood up. 'Come and see the book.'

She looked up questioningly and he held out his hand to her.

Eloise let her fingers slide inside his, intensely aware of the feeling of his hand wrapped around hers. 'I'd like to see it.'

'The library is through here.' He pointed to the double doors.

Eloise was vaguely aware of the nineteenth century mouldings, but mostly she was conscious of being with Jem.

A nice man—doing well by the people he loved. In the back she could hear the soft murmur of conversation, the words blurred.

'Laurence has a study off here,' Jem said, releasing her hand and pulling open the heavy doors. 'If he hadn't been born to this inheritance I'm sure he'd have lost himself in academia.'

'His work is well thought of,' Eloise said, hating herself for the controlled primness of her remark. And then, 'I looked it up. It's considered a definitive study.'

She looked up to find him smiling at her. 'He gets pretty little respect for it within the family.'

'Why didn't he write anything else?'

'Lack of time, I suspect. Keeping Coldwaltham Abbey solvent is a full-time job, and something of a thankless one. I don't envy him it. Or Alex.'

'He'll inherit?'

'Unless the law is changed and Belinda gets the honours.' He reached up and pulled down a hardback volume. 'Here it is. It has pride of place among original editions of Dickens and Keats.'

Eloise reached out and opened the first page.

To Nessa. With love.

There in black and white. It wasn't a wedding ring but it was a public avowal nonetheless. Proof that her mother had been loved.

She'd been the product of love.

'Did his wife—his first wife—mind it being dedicated like this?' she asked, smoothing her fingers over the words.

'I don't think she knew. By the time this was printed Sylvia was past caring about anything.'

But his daughter would have known. 'Poor Belinda,' Eloise remarked, closing the book and handing it back to him.

He turned it over in his hands. 'I have a copy at home. I'll lend it to you.'

She shook her head. 'No need. I've found a second-hand copy on the Internet. It should arrive any day.'

Jem reached up and put the slim volume back in its slot. She was glad now that she'd taken the trouble to find a copy for herself. The words of the inscription would always be proof that her mum had been loved.

That mattered so much. She'd never been comfortable with the idea of being an accident. Unwanted. A problem to be managed. Her grandma's crippling embarrassment at her daughter's lack of a husband had registered somewhere.

However much it was possible to rationalise one's childhood, it didn't change the emotional scarring. She would always be the product of her upbringing.

As would Belinda. It must hurt her to read an inscription like that. Laurence's precious book dedicated not to her mother, not to her—but to the woman her father had loved.

'Does Belinda still hate me?'

'We haven't spoken about it.'

'But…?'

'I imagine she'll find you difficult.' He reached out and took hold of her hands. 'It's not you, it's not personal. Surely you can imagine how she'd feel?' His thumb moved across the palm of her hand.

'I—I shouldn't have come.'

'I'm glad you did.'

She looked up. 'Really?'

Jem let go of her hands. 'Of course. Truth is never something to be afraid of.'

'Sometimes it hurts, though.'

'Sometimes it does,' he agreed.

Eloise looked out of the near window, along the long vista to the pond. 'I nearly didn't come.'

'Why?'

She turned slowly. 'I thought your mother would hate me. That—' She broke off, her words choked.

'She's not like that.'

And she wasn't. Marie had been warm and lovely, seemingly able to accept her arrival in her husband's life with no great trauma—and yet Jem had felt the need to protect her. She was sure of it.

'But,' Eloise began, confused, 'you hated the idea of me. You were so certain…' Her voice wavered.

Jem moved forward and gently wrapped his arms around her. Her head rested against the steady beat of his heart. 'It has nothing to do with you.'

'No?'

He pulled away and tilted her face so he could see into her eyes. 'It has far more to do with me,' he said at last.

'I don't understand.'

And Jem didn't want to explain. She'd been right when she'd said some things were too painful to be spoken of. Putting into words how he felt about his father made it all seem more real somehow.

From the moment he'd read her letter he'd had a sense that history was repeating itself. It had been a sharp reminder of all the deceit and lies that had been so much a part of his childhood.

It was him who couldn't cope with Laurence's betrayal of his sick wife and daughter. His mother had shed a few tears, more out of shock than anything else, but it was him who found Laurence's frailty difficult to come to terms with.

None of it was Eloise's fault. He knew that. But the fact of her, that she existed, had taken away the blind faith he'd always had in his stepfather.

And yet she was a victim too. Eloise had grown up without a father. Without any knowledge of who her father was.

His arms tightened around her. The feel of her hair was soft on his hands, her body warm—and he wanted to kiss her. Her beautiful face was etched with emotion and he wanted to smooth away the wrinkle on her forehead and kiss away the pain.

Jem stepped back. It was too soon. And she was too vulnerable. Too preoccupied with everything else going on in her life.

Besides, he wasn't sure what he wanted—or what her reaction would be. He pulled a hand across the back of his neck, easing out the tension.

His reaction to Eloise confused him. Outwardly she

was so cool, so controlled, and yet she didn't seem that way to him. He had an overwhelming desire to protect her, to shield her from the bitter winds of life and make everything sweet for her.

He watched as she wrapped her arms around her waist, her body stiff and nervous. He knew how difficult this was for her, how much courage she'd needed to come to Coldwaltham Abbey again.

Laurence's delight in his unexpected child was obvious, but Eloise was no fool. She'd know how difficult that would be for Belinda. Her behaviour in striking Eloise had been inexcusable but he understood the motivation. The anger.

Presumably so did Eloise, because she hadn't told Laurence. The older man obviously had no knowledge of his elder daughter's outburst.

He glanced down at his Rolex watch. 'We'd better go back. Belinda and Piers must have arrived by now.'

'Yes.' She looked nervously back at the bookshelves as though she hoped there'd be something to detain them.

'She's had more time to become accustomed to the idea of you.'

Eloise turned back and looked at him, her brown eyes luminous. 'You mean she won't slap me this time?'

'I think that's unlikely,' he answered with a small smile.

He held out his hand and she took it. Jem carefully threaded his fingers through hers. Her skin was so pale against his own, her nails perfect ovals. He pulled his gaze up to her eyes. 'If she does, I promise to leap across the scallops and rescue you.'

She gave a small giggle of laughter. 'Would you do that?'

'Absolutely.'

He led her towards the door, before releasing her hand and guiding her in front of him. Eloise hesitated in the doorway. A cursory glance around the room told her that Belinda had arrived. She was seated on a high-backed chair, her face flushed and angry.

Unconsciously, Eloise lifted her chin and she walked a little taller. She felt Jem place his hand in the middle of her back, the warmth from his fingers spreading through her body. She was glad he was there. Strong. Supportive.

'Eloise.' The Viscount came to meet her. 'I'd like you to meet my daughter, Belinda.'

Belinda's eyes looked up, a mixture of scorn and fear in their greeny-blue depths.

Eloise knew why and felt a wave of empathy, real and tangible. The kind that binds you to another soul for as long as you live.

Belinda might be forty now, but inside she was the frightened teenager she'd been all those years before.

Back then it must have felt as if her world was ending. Her mother was dying, her father had fallen in love with someone else. Belinda had been alone. Very, very alone.

It made Eloise glad she'd said nothing to her father about meeting Belinda. On their second telephone conversation he'd said how much he hoped his daughters would become friends in time and Eloise had said nothing.

That would be their secret. Eloise held out her hand with a composed smile. 'It's lovely to meet you.'

There was a flash of something. Gratitude, perhaps? She wasn't entirely certain, but Belinda took the outstretched hand in her own cold one. 'Hello.' Then her expression changed. It was like a sheet of steel coming down between them. 'I remember your mother.'

Eloise sensed Jem move closer.

'You look very like her.'

'Thank you,' Eloise replied, although she knew it hadn't been intended as a compliment.

Laurence interrupted, drawing her attention to the handsome man standing beside the mantelpiece. 'And this is Belinda's husband, Piers Atherton.'

'How do you do?' Eloise said politely, disliking the man instinctively. She couldn't say precisely why, but there was a sliminess about him that made her uneasy.

Piers took her hand in both his. 'It's a pleasure to meet you.'

His eyes said far more. They were lascivious and openly sexual. It made her feel she'd have been more comfortable if she'd chosen to wear a dress with a much higher neckline in an unbecoming shade of fuchsia.

Eloise itched to pull her hand away. She glanced back at Belinda and wondered why she had married a man like Piers. If her father's affair had caused her pain, it was strange that she'd married a man who clearly was open to suggestions.

'Shall we go through to lunch?' Marie said in her gentle French accent. 'Now we are all together.'

Belinda stood up abruptly as though she wanted the whole thing to be over. Eloise hung back until she felt Piers's fingers stroke along the length of her arm.

Under normal circumstances she would have slapped him off and told him exactly where to go, but these were hardly normal circumstances.

'I'll show you the way to the Dining Room.' Jem spoke at her elbow.

Gratefully, she turned and followed him out into the long corridor. One glance at Jem's face told her his intervention hadn't been accidental. He didn't like Piers.

For a moment they were alone and she whispered, 'Thank you.'

As the others joined them she was almost certain she heard him say, 'You're welcome.'

The Dining Room was less intimidating than she'd imagined it would be. Instead of a long formal table it was a more intimate circle. Although it still sat an easy twelve it had a homely feel.

'Eloise, if you sit beside Laurence,' Marie said with an expressive wave of her hand, 'and Jeremy beside you…you will have the two people you know best near you.'

Eloise smiled with real gratitude and sat where she'd been directed. While everyone else arranged themselves she took in the muted decorations, the heavily starched linen tablecloth and the tasteful arrangement of blood-red roses in the centre of the table. It was a far cry from her childhood.

She couldn't imagine her mum in a place like this. Had she been desperately overawed or had she loved the luxury and beauty? Was that why she'd begun an affair with a much older married man? She must have known it was wrong.

She didn't like to think about that. It was easier…more comfortable…to think of her mum as being the wronged woman, but actually that position could only fairly be occupied by Belinda's mother.

Eloise suddenly became aware that she'd been spoken to. 'I'm sorry? I was daydreaming.'

Marie smiled. 'It wasn't anything important. I was merely saying I hope you like scallops. They are Laurence's favourite and have become something of a birthday tradition.'

'Yes. Yes, I do.'

The meal dragged on interminably. It passed in a blur of Scallops with Black Peppered Tangerines, Duck with Juniper Onions and Pears and finished with a triumphant Chocolate and Date Tiramisu.

The food was exquisite, but Eloise couldn't help but think wistfully back to her family tradition of a mountain of chocolate brownies lit with candles. The formality was oppressive and the conversation laboured.

She sipped her Kahlua, perfectly chosen to accompany the dessert, and willed the meal to be over. Laurence appeared to be oblivious to the undercurrents around his table. He smiled benignly at them all, choosing to ignore the silence of his elder daughter, the inappropriate remarks made by his son-in-law and the discomfort of his son.

Alex seemed a nice young man. He was slightly diffident and certainly quiet. Marie was a superb hostess. She was elegant, intelligent and a genuinely lovely person. Often she would look to Jem for support and with innate good breeding he supported her.

It was interesting. She let the conversation, stilted though it was, happen around her. She learnt of Laurence's concerns about the damage to the Abbey's roof during the Christmas storms, about Alexander's difficulty with French, about Jem's autumn launch of directional furniture…

Marie smiled her thanks at the uniformed woman who took away her plate. 'I think coffee in the Sitting Room?'

There was a general murmur of assent and within minutes Eloise found herself back in the Winter Sitting Room, the ornate clock on the mantelpiece ticking the silence.

Belinda had brought her wineglass with her. She sat

on the left-hand sofa and fixed Eloise with a look of dislike. 'You've not said much.'

'Belinda!' her father interjected.

Her husband's mouth curled. 'She's had too much to drink.'

'What would you like to know?' Eloise answered quietly. Belinda had been steadily drinking throughout the meal, her unhappiness obvious. It didn't matter how much she told herself she wasn't to blame, she still felt guilty. Responsible for the other woman's unhappiness.

Belinda shrugged. 'I don't know. Perhaps something about your life. You live in London, don't you?'

'In Hammersmith.'

'And, before that, Birmingham? I'm sure that's what Daddy told us.'

Eloise nodded.

'You don't have the accent.'

'No.' It didn't seem worth explaining much about her childhood, the elocution lessons her mum had insisted upon, the public speaking trophies that had sat on the shelf in the lounge. Belinda wasn't genuinely interested and her questions were only making everyone else uncomfortable.

Belinda crossed her legs and swirled the wine in her glass. 'Did your mother work?'

'She was a secretary.'

'Really? I'd heard she was a cleaner.'

Eloise didn't flinch. 'That, too, if money was tight. Sometimes I went to help and earned myself some pocket money.'

'Ah, coffee,' Marie said with relief as the tray was brought in and set before her. 'How do you like your coffee, Eloise?'

'White. One sugar.' She accepted her cup with grateful

thanks and spooned out the sugar crystals with a spoon she felt certain was silver. The interruption led the conversation off in different innocuous directions.

Belinda spoke about people and places she'd never heard of. Eloise felt sure it was a deliberate ploy to demonstrate how much the outsider she was, but the most painful thing was the way the older woman refused to make eye contact. She could have been invisible.

All at once Eloise felt as though a twig had snapped inside her and she knew she'd reached the point where she couldn't cope with being here any longer. Everything about Coldwaltham Abbey was a strain: the house, the furniture, the paintings, the people.

She didn't belong here. Perhaps this was how her mum had felt in the end? Maybe that was why she'd thought it better not to try and make contact?

Jem was there to take away her empty cup, his fingers lightly brushing against hers.

'I'd better go,' she said, watching as he placed it carefully on the tray.

Marie looked at her son and back at Eloise. 'Are you driving back to London tonight?'

Eloise deliberately didn't answer. The truth was that she'd booked herself into a nearby hotel, but the prospect of being offered a bed at Coldwaltham Abbey terrified her. She wasn't ready for that—either for herself or for Belinda.

She glanced across at the other woman. It was strange to feel so much compassion for someone who so obviously didn't like her. But then they were sisters. It was an idea that was gong to take some getting used to.

In her peripheral vision, Eloise saw Marie speak quietly to her elder son and noticed his slight nod of agreement. Then the older woman turned back to her and asked, 'Perhaps Jeremy could show you something of the Abbey grounds before you have to leave Sussex?'

Jem looked across at her. 'I could do with some fresh air. Would you like a walk?'

'I—I'm not…' Eloise floundered. Then, 'Yes, I'd like that.' There was no reason to refuse. 'A walk would be lovely.'

Within seconds she was standing on the steps, her goodbyes said. The wind whipped round the front of the Abbey and Eloise pulled her lambswool coat closely round her body.

Jem looked up at the sky. 'It's going to be cold.'

'Yes.'

'My mother was concerned that Belinda might have upset you. She doesn't want you to leave Coldwaltham unhappy.'

Eloise forced a smile. 'I'm not.'

He looked across at her. 'Do you want this walk?'

The air contracted around her. She did. The prospect of walking with Jem was immediately appealing. She might try and tell herself it was because she didn't want to be alone in a hotel room, but she knew better.

Being with Jem wasn't wise. She didn't belong here and she ought to leave.

'Is it too much trouble?'

He smiled, deep grooves appearing beside his mouth. 'It's no trouble at all.'

CHAPTER SEVEN

THEY walked down the steps and started to follow the long path. Jem pushed his hands deep in his overcoat pockets, then lifted his face and studied the grey sky. 'Belinda was very rude.'

'I was expecting it. I probably shouldn't have come,' she said, her smile twisting, 'but I couldn't resist it. I've never had a father before.'

'Laurence was glad you came.'

'Was he?'

Jem's face softened and he turned to look at her. 'You've been his ray of sunlight. His bypass operation has really taken it out of him. He says it's the most painful thing he's ever had to endure.'

'Oh.'

'My mother's been very scared.' They walked through the courtyard and Jem steered her towards an archway on the right. 'You've not got the right footwear for heavy walking. We'd better stick to the main tourist route.'

In her three-inch high stilettos Eloise was grateful for the wide flagged path. The wind caught at the hem of her dress and blew it against her legs. 'When did Coldwaltham Abbey open to the public?'

'1948. Like many big houses it's struggled for survival since the Second World War.'

'That doesn't seem right.' And then, suddenly, 'Does Belinda have a drink problem?'

'She has a drink problem. A self-esteem problem.' Jem

glanced across at her, gauging her reaction. 'A husband problem.'

'Piers is a bit of a slime ball.'

Jem gave a crack of laughter. 'You noticed.'

'Difficult to miss. Cassie, my editor-in-chief, would describe him as a "stroker". Why does she stay married to him?'

He shrugged. 'Who knows? She was brought up under Laurence's aegis; perhaps she thinks marriage is insoluble?' A silence stretched between them, and then he added, 'I'm sorry, that was insensitive of me. I shouldn't have said that to you. I—'

'He clearly did think marriage was for keeps,' Eloise interrupted. She turned and looked back at the house, the mellow walls covered with roses and wisteria. 'I wish Mum had told me. I don't know why she didn't. We had such a good relationship…'

Eloise fumbled in her pocket, searching for a tissue. She brought one out and dabbed at her eyes.

Jem looked away, his eyes still focused on the house. 'She died very suddenly. She might have intended to tell you…later.'

'How much later? I was twenty-one when she died, for heaven's sake. It's not as though it's such a shameful secret, is it?' She balled the tissue up angrily. 'Or perhaps it is. Damn! What they did to Belinda is pretty shameful. I wonder if anyone was thinking about her.'

'You're a very unusual woman,' he said, turning towards her with his slow smile.

'Why? I'm only telling the truth.'

His smile deepened. 'I'd say that was fairly unusual. Not many people can face reality without filtering the glare somehow.'

Together they turned and passed through wrought iron

gates framed by vast leaves. 'I wish she'd told me. There are so many things I want to know, but I don't know Laurence well enough to ask.'

'Like?'

'Like what did they say to each other on that last day. They must have known his wife was dying. Why didn't they plan on meeting up later? Why didn't Mum tell Laurence she was expecting me? Why didn't she contact him after his wife died? It doesn't make sense, does it?'

It didn't. But then neither did the affair in the first place. Everything Jem had ever known about Laurence would have suggested such a thing was impossible. His stepfather's opinions were fixed and unalterable.

He was aware of Eloise turning to look at him. 'Don't you think it's odd they didn't keep in contact? They didn't seem to have had a row. Nothing. So why?'

'You never really know what's going on in other people's lives,' Jem replied carefully.

'That sounds personal.'

'It is.' They turned and approached the South Lawn. It was incredibly personal. His mother had lived a lie to the outside world. His father. He'd watched the lies and the deceit play out until his father's death. He'd witnessed the incredible hurt one human being could inflict on another.

Nothing much surprised him any more. Piers's treatment of Belinda was despicable and yet she seemed powerless to walk away. Her personality had been ground down, much like his own mother's had been. He'd seen it before. Two people who'd promised to love each other and yet did everything they could to hurt and to wound.

But Laurence…

That had cut him where it hurt. Almost, almost he'd believed it was possible to live life on a higher plane.

'There's the tree,' he said, with a nod at an old oak tree in the centre of a sprawling lawn.

Eloise looked up questioningly.

'The tree in the photograph you gave me. Of your mother. That's the tree in the background.'

Ignoring the softness of the grass and the way her heels dipped in the mud, Eloise walked towards it. Her hands reached out and touched the craggy bark. 'Here?'

'Don't you recognise it?'

Eloise let her eyes follow a path back to the house. The South Front of the house had large symmetrical windows all along its length, making the most of the long vista down to the Church. 'They certainly weren't skulking in corners, were they? Do you think people knew?'

'With staff around...Belinda...I can't imagine their affair went undetected.'

'Did her mother?'

'It's possible. Perhaps Sylvia was too ill to notice.'

That didn't seem likely. Eloise leant back against the broad trunk and closed her eyes, shutting out the intrusive image of a dying woman watching. Hurting.

It was uncomfortable to have to think of her mum as less than perfect. She had such a sanctified image of her. She'd been so loving, so supportive...such a wonderful person.

She desperately wanted to cling to all of that. To remember all the good times, treasure up every precious memory. Of course, all of that was still true. It was just that there were other facets of her mum's life she hadn't known about.

It changed things. Shifted her perspective slightly. With new information she had to filter all her perceptions a little differently.

Her mum no longer seemed a pawn in a rich man's

game. No passive participant in her misfortune. She'd made wrong choices. She had been human with her share of human frailty. Eloise wished she'd been given the chance to say she understood.

She opened her eyes and turned to look at Jem. He hadn't moved; his blue eyes were watching her. Slowly he reached out and touched the bark of the tree, his fingers almost reverent.

Eloise watched as they spread out. He wasn't at all the way she'd imagined he'd be. There was an innate strength about him. He made you believe he could be trusted.

'If you want to see any more of the garden we ought to get going. The light is fading.'

They turned and walked back to the path, following it as far as the espaliered apple trees. The scale of the place was mind-blowing.

Jem followed the line of her gaze and remarked, 'Those two beds are used for growing cut flowers. There's a band of ladies who produce all the arrangements through the house. Every Friday.'

'That's quite a commitment.'

'Coldwaltham inspires great love.' Jem pulled a face at the steadily darkening sky. 'We can't be much longer.'

Eloise took her mobile phone out of her handbag. 'I'd better ring for a taxi. I'm staying overnight in Arundel.'

'With friends?'

She stopped searching through the pre-programmed numbers and looked up. 'Actually, no.' She hesitated. 'I don't like driving at night.' Jem's eyebrows shot up. 'Stupid, I know. I've never liked it much, but since mum's accident...' She shrugged and continued searching for the number of the local taxi firm.

He laid a hand over hers. 'It doesn't sound stupid at all.'

Her fingers stilled and she looked directly into his blue eyes. Nice eyes. Nice man.

It had been such a long time since she'd thought that about a man. So many games, so many hidden agendas, but with Jem it was different. He really was genuine.

He let his hand fall away. 'If you're not rushing back to London… I've got something to show you.'

'What?'

'Wait and see.'

Eloise put her mobile back in the side pocket of her handbag and they cut through the herb garden and back out to the long central path.

Coldwaltham Abbey rose up majestically from behind the high yew hedge. It was all so beautiful, steeped in history. It felt so permanent. Something to belong to.

Eloise turned back to look at it and caught sight of Jem's expression. It was a mixture of pride and contentment. He really loved this place.

His words echoed in her head. *Coldwaltham inspires great love.*

The thought came as a shock. She'd always imagined the people who lived in these kinds of houses loved them as a possession, but Jem seemed to be really connected to the house. It showed on his face and reverberated in his voice. Perhaps that was why he stayed?

Would she have felt like that if she'd been brought up in Coldwaltham Abbey? It would be wonderful to feel connected to a place. To feel your roots firmly established with friends and family about you.

It seemed very unlikely that would ever be her lot. She'd discovered that today. You couldn't just adopt a family. It came from years of belonging, of knowing you were working together for the good of each other. She would always be the outsider here. Her presence would always cause Belinda huge pain.

Eloise turned away from the house and scanned Jem's profile. He had a quiet, intelligent face. It was difficult to imagine him as a rebellious teenager, kicking out against the world.

'What are you going to show me?' she asked quickly as he caught her staring.

'My pet project. I think you'll like it.'

She frowned but he wouldn't say any more. He led her to the small gravelled courtyard where he'd left his Land Rover.

'Where are we going?'

Jem smiled. 'It's not far, but too long a walk in heels like that.'

She glanced down at her feet. Shoes were such a weakness. She loved the soft creamy leather, the high twisted heels. It was almost as though he could read her mind because his blue eyes were laughing when she looked up. A sinful glint that stopped her breath in her throat and made the air freeze around her.

'You should read my column. They give a great shape to calves.'

'Who needs heels?' he shot back.

Eloise felt as if she was in free fall. The air swirled around her, colours blurred and Cassie's words reverberated in her head. *Sexy. So very sexy.*

His eyes caressed her. Teased her. *This was a mistake.* She ought to plead a headache and leave now.

'Shall we go?' He stood with the Land Rover door held open.

Eloise jerked into life. She climbed up into the worn seat, aware of the way her skirt rode up, displaying a length of creamy thigh. Without looking at him, she quickly slid the soft folds of her dress back into place. Outwardly she was the picture of cool control, but internally she was a whirling inferno.

She'd never been so confused by a man. Had never been so uncertain what she wanted from him. Did she want him to kiss her? Hold her? Make love to her?

Had this been how her mum had felt about Laurence? Maybe it was Coldwaltham Abbey itself that wove the magic?

Jem settled himself in the driver's seat, his movements smooth and unflustered. But she'd seen the flash of desire in his eyes. Whatever he said, whatever he did, she knew their attraction was mutual.

And unexpected. How could two people from such dissimilar backgrounds find any common ground?

And impossible. They weren't merely two strangers, free to like each other or not at will. She was the illegitimate daughter of his mother's husband. It was an invisible barrier between them; neither would risk crossing it. The stakes were too high.

It was all so wrong. She would see what Jem wanted to show her—and then she'd leave. Not just now, but leave for good. She didn't belong with these people. If she stayed she would only get hurt.

Jem drove past all the landmarks she recognised. She turned away from the window. 'Where are we?'

'Still on the Coldwaltham estate,' he answered, shifting gear for a tight bend. 'And this…is my baby.'

He stopped outside a converted barn. Large glass windows dominated the front and Eloise turned to stare down at the view.

'It's incredible, isn't it?' he murmured at her elbow.

'There's Windmill Hill, which takes you back to the Abbey, and all around are the Downs.'

'It's breathtaking.'

'As soon as I saw this place I knew I had to do something with it. It's taken years for the planning department to agree.'

Eloise tore her eyes away from the view. 'It's yours?'

'All mine. Laurence gave it to me on my twenty-first birthday, but I only got permission to convert it to a dwelling last year. I'm eight months in and it's just about habitable.'

As he spoke he led her through the heavy front doors and into a high, galleried entrance hall. The scale of it was immense but the central area was dominated by a large, circular table.

Eloise stepped forward and stroked her hand across the fine grain of the wood. The movement echoed a memory and she turned back to look at him. 'This is the table you were making? In your workshop?'

'That's my Arthurian Table. I wanted something that would really make a statement. It's a demanding space.'

Eloise let her eyes scan the incredible beauty of the piece, the exquisite craftsmanship. The wide, circular top had been divided into segments. In each segment was a word—a virtue—picked out in contrasting woods.

She traced a finger across the word 'Honour'. 'What do they call this technique? Is it marquetry?'

'That's right. It's never going to catch on as a commercially produced piece, far too expensive to make, but it was a real labour of love.'

They were all there. 'Faith', 'Hope', 'Peace', 'Love', 'Valour'…

'How did you think of this?'

Jem coaxed her further inside. 'Put it down to too

many fantasy novels as a child. I loved all the tales of King Arthur and the Knights of the Round Table. It's just a grown-up version.'

It was more than that. Just a few short months ago she would have written him off as a parasite. Someone who'd got where he was purely by dint of being connected to the right people.

But Jem Norland had talent. Real, discernible brilliance in his chosen field. He couldn't help the circumstances of his birth any more than she could hers.

Her mum had always said a person's responsibility was to use their talents and opportunities as well as they possibly could. He had done just that. How irritating it must be to him to have his achievements disregarded merely because he was born to money.

'What are you thinking?' he asked.

Eloise spun round. 'You're really good at this.'

'And you're surprised?'

Yes. No.

He smiled at her hesitation. 'Yes, I'm good at this. But without my father's money I might never have got started.'

'How did you know I was thinking that?'

His feet echoed on the wooden floors. 'You and everyone else. I've always been battling to prove myself.'

'I'm sorry.'

He shrugged. 'Come and see the kitchen. It's not quite finished. I've still to make some of the cupboards, but you can see the idea.'

The kitchen was a pale maple, startling against the dark granite worktops.

'What do you think?'

'It's incredible. The whole place. No wonder you dislike being in London.'

Jem set a kettle to boil on the Aga. 'Tea? Coffee?'

'Tea, please.' Eloise spun round to take in the full impact of the huge open-plan living-kitchen-informal dining room. It was spectacular. The floor was an endless expanse of wide floorboards with a rich patina.

'I admit the floor was a bit of a find,' he said, following the line of her eyes. 'I managed to source it from an old hospital that was being demolished in Aberdeenshire. Then I had to arrange for it to be transported down here.'

'It's reclaimed?'

Jem poured water into a hand-thrown teapot. 'A new floor wouldn't have worked here. Sourcing old materials is a time-consuming business, but this place is a labour of love.'

'Your pet project,' Eloise echoed, smiling even though she felt herself falling deeper under his spell. It was impossible not to.

'Nothing's allowed here if I don't love it. The mugs,' he said, holding up a pottery mug in a cobalt blue, 'were made by Saskia Kemsley.'

'I've heard of her.'

Jem poured in the tea. 'Her pieces sell in Harrods, but she's a local girl with a pottery a couple of miles outside of Chichester.' He handed her a mug and indicated one of the large modernist sofas in a pale cream.

She sat down and wrapped her hands round the pottery mug. Through the large picture window she could see the light dip and fade until the view became lost in blackness. There was a curious peace about it.

Even their silence was companionable. Eloise looked across at Jem, his head resting against the back of the sofa. He looked tired, as though the day had been as stressful to him as it had been to her.

She noticed the small lines fanning out at the edges of

his eyes, the small slivers of silver in his hair. He opened one eye.

'I—I ought to be going,' Eloise said, hurriedly looking away and putting her mug down on the maple coffee table in front of her.

'Why?'

There was no reason she cared to explain. Nothing and no one to go back to. 'It's late,' she managed lamely.

'Not very. I don't have much food in the house but I can probably rustle us up an omelette.'

'But—'

'I can drive you into Arundel later. When I go home myself.'

Eloise frowned. 'Don't you live here?'

'Not yet.' Jem stood up and reached down for her mug. 'I'm still at the cottage. There are no beds here yet and the bathrooms only went in last week.'

He wandered across to the fridge. 'Omelettes are a definite possibility. I can even manage cheese. Plus,' he said pulling a bottle of white wine from the wine cooler, 'I've got a nice bottle of Chardonnay. What do you say?'

Eloise glanced down at her watch. It was still so early, the evening stretched out before her. And the alternative was so tempting. *Would it really matter?*

'I'll certainly stay for the Chardonnay.'

'Good girl!'

She watched as he broke the eggs into a bowl and lightly beat them with a fork.

'How long have you lived in London?' he asked.

'Since I finished at uni. That's over six years now.'

'You didn't go back home?'

'I didn't have a home to go back to.'

Jem glanced across at her. 'I suppose not. Nice you and Laurence both went to Cambridge.'

Eloise looked down at the colours in the granite, touches of blue and grey mixed in with the black. 'It must be so strange for him to suddenly find he has a daughter he's known nothing about.'

Jem poured the eggs into a hot frying pan and tilted it so the eggs covered the base of the pan. His eyes watched for the optimum moment before he drew a palette knife through the soft mixture, making a channel.

He looked across at her intently watching him. 'Do you cook?'

'Never.'

'Why?'

'It's never occurred to me to try, I suppose,' she said slowly.

He flipped the omelette out on to a plate, before pouring out a large glass of wine. 'We'll have to eat on our laps; I've not made the chairs yet.'

Foolish it might be, but Eloise had never felt so happy. She felt comfortable, settled and completely at home. She took her plate and wine across to the place she'd sat before and slipped off her shoes.

A minute later, Jem walked over to join her.

'Aren't you drinking?' she asked, noticing his iced water.

'I've got to drive home.'

'You shouldn't have opened the bottle for me.'

'Why ever not?' He sat down opposite her, precariously placing his glass at his feet. 'I can't decide what I want to do with the chairs. Do I go for something timeless or something dramatic?'

'Dramatic. No doubt about it,' Eloise replied, giving up and sipping her wine. 'With a room like that, you've not got any choice about it.'

Jem laughed and put his plate down on the floor.

'You'd better have a look at these.' He walked over and pulled open one of the kitchen drawers. Tucked inside a black folder were sheets of design ideas, some no more than outline sketches, others had been shaded and construction points noted.

'I like this one,' Eloise said after a moment. 'That one's too Gothic, but this one has the height and I love the asymmetric back rest.'

He took the paper from her hand. 'Difficult to get the curve, but...'

'How did you start?' Eloise asked curiously, watching the intent look on his face as he studied his design.

Jem carefully placed the drawing back on the top of the papers in his file. 'I began shortly after I came to live here. At Coldwaltham. I was allowed to use off-cuts of wood from projects that were going on around the Abbey. Given the space to do it.'

'But you're not self-taught?'

'Wasn't that in your research?'

Eloise had almost forgotten about her Internet searches. They'd given the merest outline, the facts, but they'd actually told her nothing about the man in any real sense.

She frowned, concentrating. 'You've got a degree in design.'

'Very good.' His blue eyes glinted over the top of his water glass.

'A first. I can't remember from where.'

His mouth twitched.

'You weren't the primary focus of my research!'

Jem gave a crack of laughter. 'I suppose not. After I graduated, I found myself a top rate apprenticeship and really learnt how to work with wood.'

He smiled. 'There are some advantages in not having

to earn a living. I had nothing to do but follow my own inclinations.'

'That's lovely.'

He shook his head. 'I was lucky to find something I love doing. It could all have been very different. When I arrived at Coldwaltham I was set to go very wrong. I'd the money to finance it too.'

Eloise sipped her chilled alcohol, letting the flavours fill her mouth. 'What changed things?'

'Laurence.'

The silence pooled softly. Eloise finished her omelette and carefully placed her knife and fork together.

'Do you want to know why I resented you so much? When I first met you?' he asked suddenly.

Eloise nodded.

'Because it meant Laurence isn't better than any other man.' Jem walked over and refilled his water glass. 'Do you need a refill?'

Eloise shook her head, her blonde hair swinging.

He'd no idea why he wanted to tell her; he only knew that he did. She was so restful, her graceful fingers linked loosely round the stem of her wineglass.

'My father was a bully.' He saw the slight widening of her brown eyes. It gave him some satisfaction to know that he'd shocked her.

It gave him even more to actually say the words out loud. For years he'd kept his feelings locked inside him. It had seemed wrong to denigrate a man who was no longer alive to defend himself and with complete cowardice he preferred to shutter the past firmly away, pretend it had all been part of another lifetime.

But his father's legacy lived on—not just the financial one but the emotional one too.

'A cheat, a liar and a bully,' he said with controlled deliberation.

'Rupert Norland?' Eloise's voice held the faintest trace of a question.

He couldn't blame her for that. The whole world had a completely different image of the successful, charming entrepreneur. Women had loved him and men had admired him. They'd had no idea how the man had transformed once he'd been at home.

As soon as the front door shut his charming visage had vanished and you'd been left with a brute of a man. A man who, when the pressure rose, had vented his spleen with his fists.

He'd grown up seeing his mother cowering in the corner and carefully concealing the bruises on her arms and legs. His father had been careful never to leave a mark where it could be seen.

He'd watched as his mother's personality had slowly been eroded until she was too fearful to do anything but stay. And Jem had grown up knowing what it was to feel completely powerless.

'Things aren't always what they seem,' he said quietly. 'When Laurence fell in love with my mother he was so gentle with her. So patient. I admired him for it, even though it frightened me.'

'And with you?' she said softly, her words travelling on a breath.

He felt a smile tug at the corner of his mouth, the dark images of his past vanishing. 'He'd the patience of a saint. I was a tearaway. More ready to use my fists than my tongue.'

'I've never understood that.'

Jem looked up. Two short lines were creasing the smooth skin on her forehead.

'Why do children of bullies become bullies? That was what you were saying, wasn't it?' she asked hesitantly, suddenly uncertain.

'I think,' Jem said slowly, sitting back on the sofa, 'it's because it's the only thing you've seen. You don't rationalise it, of course, you just respond to the anger inside. It's all there, bubbling away. Then it suddenly erupts uncontrollably.'

'Was that why you got expelled?'

Jem nodded. 'For that, and for bringing into school an illegal stash of cigarettes.'

'Was that after you were living at Coldwaltham?'

'The expulsion was. Everyone had really reached the end of their tether with me by then. My father's death had been sudden, so people tended to make allowances, but then I broke another boy's front tooth and they couldn't ignore my behaviour any longer.'

Eloise moved slightly and her hair shone in the light like softly spun gold. She was almost not human. Perhaps that was why he felt able to open up his soul to her.

Maybe it was because he knew she understood something of loss.

'What did Laurence do?'

Do? He'd never put that in words before. He'd done everything and nothing. 'He listened,' Jem said at last. 'He seemed to like me and he believed in me.'

Eloise smiled and the effect was incandescent. It lit her face as though she were divine. 'My mum did that for me. I could talk to her about anything…'

She trailed off, her face shadowed.

'Which is why it hurts so much that she didn't tell you about Laurence?' he suggested.

She gently bowed her head, her hair shielding her face.

'They're not perfect,' he said softly. 'Not Laurence. Not your mum.'

'No.' She looked up. 'I do know that. I just wish…'

The air crackled between them, whatever she'd been about to say forgotten. Jem felt as if he was being drawn across the room by an invisible thread.

Somehow he was next to her and it was so easy. So very easy. He let his hand slide into the rich gold of her hair. It was soft and fine.

He felt the shape of her skull beneath his fingers as he drew her closer. And closer. She didn't resist him. Eloise seemed to melt beneath his fingers in a way she'd only done in his dreams.

She came to him as naturally as if there was no other place in the world she wanted to be. Her body curved towards him and her lips parted. Blood surged in his ears and he forgot how foolish this was. Forgot every resolution he'd made.

Her lips moved beneath his. Impossibly sweet. Her hands snaked round his neck and her fingers buried themselves in his hair. He heard the soft murmur in her throat, felt her body relax against his.

There was a sense of inevitability about it. The small voice of caution had long since been silenced. There was only her and his great need of her.

Love?

All his life he'd avoided this intensity of feeling. The need to be in control was paramount. He would never, could never, trust another human being with his happiness. He'd seen too much. Hurt too much.

But, with Eloise, it felt right.

The paralysing fear was gone and in its place was a sense of wonder. A feeling that the world was no longer out of kilter, but in perfect alignment.

'Eloise,' he murmured helplessly against her throat.

Jem felt her hands still and then uncurl from his hair. It was a moment of utter despair. She was pulling away from him, not just physically but emotionally.

'This isn't…it isn't a good idea.'

His hands fell to his sides as though they were made of lead.

'I can't do this. I'm so sorry.' She turned away in agitation.

Her hair was ruffled, her lips swollen from his kisses—and Jem felt as if his world had ended. 'Why?'

Eloise looked up at him, her eyes gleaming with unshed tears. 'I shouldn't…we shouldn't…' She turned round and searched for her shoes. 'I'll ring for a taxi.'

'I'll drive you.'

'I can't—'

Jem reached out and held her by the shoulders, forcing her to meet his eyes. 'I don't pretend to understand why we can't, but I respect your decision.' Even though it killed him to say it. 'I'll drive you to Arundel.'

'Thank you,' she said, backing away. 'It's just not a good idea. With Laurence. Belinda.'

He watched as she slipped her stilettos on and reached for her long cream coat. Slowly he picked up his own jacket and felt in the pockets for the keys to his Land Rover.

Her lips trembled as she tried to produce a smile. 'Shall we go?'

Jem nodded, feeling as though a knife had been twisted in his gut.

He shut the door of the barn firmly behind him, aware of the way Eloise shivered in the night air. It would have been the perfect opportunity to wrap his arms around her, tilt her face upwards and kiss her.

Instead he forced a smile. 'Let's go.'

CHAPTER EIGHT

ELOISE shut this month's issue of *Image* and sneezed into her tissue. She felt so sick. Her head felt as if it had been stuffed with cotton wool and her throat felt as if it had been shredded with razor blades.

It didn't help that Jem had just won a prestigious award for innovative design and his photograph had been featured in this month's *Image*. His personality seemed to leap directly off the page. It meant she remembered how it had felt when he'd held her. *Kissed her*.

There was no escaping it. His face even stared down from the coffee room wall at the *Image* offices because some bright spark had put it there 'because of his bedroom eyes'. And she didn't want to remember.

It had all been a terrible mistake.

She'd kissed him.

Or he'd kissed her. She couldn't remember who'd actually crossed that invisible line. The fact remained, they'd kissed.

And things would never be the same again. She would always know what it was like to be in his arms. To hear her name murmured softly against her throat.

Eloise reached for another tissue and curled up on her sofa. Laurence had been right. He'd been speaking of himself and her mum, but it all pertained to her as well. There had been so many little decisions which had led up to that life-changing moment.

She could have turned down the invitation to her father's birthday lunch. She could have left immediately afterwards and not gone on a walk around the gardens.

She could have refused Jem's offer of a lift to Arundel. She should never have gone into his house, or allowed him to make her an omelette and drink his wine.

They had seemed such little things. Each one leading naturally on to the next.

Laurence had said everything changed when he'd kissed her mum. He'd said it was the point at which they could have chosen to walk away...

They hadn't made that choice—but she had. She'd walked away.

It had been the right decision. The only decision. Eloise knew how Jem's world operated in a way her mum couldn't possibly have known.

It was a closed shop. People knew other people who knew people. It mattered who your father was, your grandfather. People networked and built dynasties.

They did *not* marry girls from Birmingham council estates or even nice suburbs. They might sleep with them, use them, but that was as far as it went.

And she didn't want that. If she'd wanted to be a rich man's plaything there had been plenty of opportunities in the past couple of years.

Jem Norland was an attractive man. Sexy. *Very, very sexy*. But she didn't want what he could offer her. She couldn't afford to let herself love him. So the only thing she could have done was walk away.

Wasn't it?

What was the matter with her? There'd been no choice. She didn't want a life like her mother's. She'd seen what that had looked like—and rejected it. It was a tough, hard road to travel. And it wasn't for her.

Jem Norland wasn't the right man for her. Everything

about his beautiful barn conversion had told her that. She didn't belong there. She *never* would belong there. And she wasn't going to think about it any more.

Eloise adjusted the cushion to make it more comfortable before abandoning the attempt and sitting up, tissue in hand, her head foggy and her nose blocked. She felt dreadful and decidedly sorry for herself.

Twenty-eight today and all she had to show for it was a particularly nasty head cold and a voucher to have her legs waxed from her colleagues at *Image*.

The buzzer to her flat managed to pierce her befuddled brain. With an inner groan Eloise picked up her roll of toilet tissue in one hand and padded across to the intercom. 'Hello?'

'Eloise?'

Even through the hazy fog of cold, Jem's voice echoed in her head. Jem was here. Now. She leant against the door frame and closed her eyes.

Oh, no. Please, no. What did he want? Why was he here?

She took a moment for the shock to subside and then pushed the button that enabled her to speak. 'Go away. I'm ill.'

'Laurence sent me.'

Eloise banged her head gently on the wall. *Laurence had sent him.* Of course; he was here because of Laurence and her birthday. It was nothing to do with her. For one moment she'd allowed herself to hope. How stupid was that?

Damn, damn and damn.

She tried again. 'I'm sick.'

'He's got you a present.' Jem's voice sounded muffled through the intercom. There was a pause and then, 'Eloise, open the door.' He sounded weary. 'It's raining.'

Reluctantly, she pushed the button to let him up. Then she looked about her lounge with growing horror. Piles of her mother's papers lay strewn about the room where she'd been making a futile attempt to go through them. Empty coffee cups sat on the side and an old worn blanket sprawled across her minimalist sofa.

She made a mad dash for the pile of tissues down the back of the sofa and gasped as she caught sight of her wan face in the mirror. There was no time to do anything. Jem rapped on the door.

Eloise clutched at her gaping dressing gown and went to open the door, stopping only to tuck the toilet roll out of sight under a cushion. She opened the door a few centimetres. 'I'm sick. Go away.'

Jem had his collar turned up against the rain and he looked irritated. 'Is it catching?'

'Yes.'

'Then don't breathe on me,' he said, pushing the door open. 'Hurry up and let me in. I'm not about to push Laurence's present through the gap.'

Eloise gave in to the inevitable. She stood back and let him come in.

'You look terrible.'

'Believe me, I feel worse.' She sunk down on the sofa and clutched a tissue to her nose.

Jem frowned. 'Who's looking after you?'

'I'm looking after myself. That's what big girls do.' She sneezed.

'Are you drinking plenty of fluids?'

Eloise looked up over the top of her tissue. 'What is this?'

It was scarily good to see him. He looked so much better than his photograph in *Image*. It had not been that long since she'd seen him, but she'd forgotten quite how tall he was, how blue his eyes were…

And last time she'd seen him she'd kissed him. Her fingers had curved into the thick black hair, her body had pressed up against his.

She watched as he unbuttoned his jacket and threw it over the chair. He didn't behave like the phenomenally rich man he was. Perhaps because he was so used to it, it didn't occur to him to think about it? Jem seemed as comfortable in her small lounge as he had in Coldwaltham Abbey's great rooms.

He hunkered down in front of her and laid a cold hand on her forehead. 'Have you got a temperature?'

'I've got a cold. It's nothing.' She pulled her dressing gown more closely round her body and tucked her feet beneath her. 'If you want a drink you'll have to make it yourself.'

'Fair enough,' he said, starting for the kitchen.

Eloise gave a squawk. 'I'll do it. What do you want?' she said, scrambling from the sofa as she remembered the state she'd left the kitchen in.

'A coffee would be great. If it's no trouble.'

She pushed past him and flicked on the kettle switch. 'I'm going to make myself a hot lemon drink anyway,' she said ungraciously. 'It'll have to be instant coffee, though. It's all I've got.'

Jem stood in the doorway and watched as she ripped open the packet of cold remedy and poured the powder into a mug.

'Go through to the lounge,' he said. 'I'll bring it through.'

For a minute she looked as if she might protest, but then she shrugged and padded back to the lounge. 'I'm too ill to argue.'

If she'd thought about it she would have expected Jem to be in London this week for the presentation of his award. She could hear the sounds of him moving about in her tiny kitchen, the sound of her fridge door being shut.

Eloise curled up in the corner of her sofa and closed her eyes. She hadn't got the energy to fight it.

Jem placed the tray on the wooden trunk. 'Be careful with the lemon; it's still very hot.'

Eloise cast him a scornful look and picked it up, cradling the mug between her hands. 'Congratulations on your award.'

'Thank you.'

'We featured it,' she said lamely, a half nod at the magazine on the trunk.

'I know.'

His eyes seemed to skim over her body as though he'd actually touched her. She felt a trailing blaze of heat alert every nerve-ending to the fact that he was here. Now. Standing in front of her. No longer a figment of her imagination.

'Why didn't you answer my calls?'

Eloise hesitated and sipped her lemon drink. Why did he think? Everything about him terrified her. Everything about love and loss and rejection terrified her too. It wasn't worth the pain. At least she knew where she was with what she'd got now. She could cope with that.

'I've been busy.'

'But not too busy to talk to Laurence.'

No, not too busy to do that.

Jem sat down opposite her and picked up his coffee. 'Or Belinda.'

Her fingers moved against the warmth of her mug.

'She telephoned me. She came up to London and we had lunch.'

'How was it?'

'What did she say?' Eloise hedged.

Jem's mouth twisted into a reluctant smile. 'She's booked into rehab.'

'Really?' Eloise looked up, her eyes finding a new sparkle. 'That's good. Really good. I'm so glad.'

She'd wondered whether Belinda would do what she'd said she would. Amazingly, she'd liked the other woman. *Her half-sister.* Would there ever be a time when that seemed a natural thought?

'Laurence is delighted.'

Eloise smiled across at him, forgetting everything else but her pleasure at the news. 'I hoped she would.'

'How have you been?' he asked softly.

Her smile faded. 'Great.' She fidgeted with the fabric of her dressing gown. 'Apart from this cold, of course.'

Jem watched the movement of her fingers. He'd almost forgotten how beguiling she was.

He hadn't thought there could be anything more alluring than the Eloise he'd already met, but he'd been wrong. Her hair was ruffled, her skin pale and her eyes bloodshot, but she still exuded a sexuality that astounded him.

Frightened him too, if he was honest. All his adult life he'd avoided intimacy. Laurence had done a lot to repair the damage of his early childhood, but even he hadn't been able to remove the fear of betrayal.

Eloise shifted slightly on the sofa and he caught a glimpse of those long—impossibly long—legs. Jem turned away and walked over to his jacket.

He no longer wondered at why Laurence had fallen in love with Nessa. It would have been like a siren's call,

impossible to resist. Every time he was with Eloise he
heard the same call. Piercingly beautiful.

All he had to do was hand over Laurence's present—
and his own—then he could leave. It could all be done
in moments and he could be on his way. He didn't even
need to stay and drink his coffee.

If that was what she wanted.

It would probably be for the best. Even Laurence
hadn't been able to remain faithful to the things he believed in. He'd been lured away by something beyond
his control.

Why should it be any different for him?

His fingers closed round the oblong package Laurence
had asked him to bring. 'Happy Birthday,' he said, turning round. 'Laurence said if you couldn't come to Sussex
I had to be his messenger and give you this.'

Eloise put the lemon drink back down on the trunk.
'For me? A present for me?'

Jem passed over the parcel, watching the shadows pass
over her face. Disbelief and then pleasure. Was she really
so alone in the world that a present was a surprise to her?

'What is it?'

'Open it.'

Eloise slid her fingers under the sticky tape and pulled
back the shiny silver paper.

'Do you speak French?' he asked, watching the bemused expression pass over her face as she saw the title
of the book Laurence had sent.

She looked up. 'Not well. At least,' she said, brushing
her hand through her hair, 'not well enough to manage
this.'

Jem deliberately chose a seat opposite her. 'It's the
story of Eloise and Abelard. Actually Heloise,' he said

in a perfect French accent. 'They were real people, apparently.'

Eloise sat with her hand resting on top of the book as though it were the most precious thing she owned. Her face took on a softness he hadn't seen before and, for the first time, he really understood how much this mattered to her.

It was about *family*. About acceptance. No one knew better than him how healing that could be. To suddenly find oneself swept up into a warm, supportive community. To belong.

Eloise needed that. Just as he'd needed it.

'Who was she?' she asked.

Jem picked up his black coffee and sipped slowly. 'Heloise was the eighteen-year-old niece and ward of a powerful churchman in eleventh century Paris. His name was Fulbert.'

'And Abelard?'

'Peter Abelard was her tutor and a philosophy scholar. Much older. That account,' he said with a nod at the book, 'places him in his forties.'

Eloise picked up the book and turned it over. 'My mum really named me with a vengeance, didn't she?'

'I don't think Laurence sees it quite like that. He sees you more like a bequest.'

A bequest? Could that really have been her mum's intention in putting that letter in with her will? Had she wanted her to get in contact with her father?

It was a beautiful theory, but Eloise couldn't quite believe it. Her mum hadn't expected to die and Laurence was...well, he was much older. She must have expected to outlive him.

Eloise knew the poem verbatim; she'd read it so often since her first visit to Sussex. The Eloise of Pope's poem lived with a lifelong regret and a yearning for the man she'd been forcibly parted from. Had that been reality for her mum?

It had been a waste of a life. And it was too late to really know. Eloise had never imagined that their time together was going to be cut short so suddenly. There were still so many answers she wanted, so many questions to ask.

The pain of it rose up and threatened to engulf her. She felt the first shuddering of grief, regret for everything that might have been. Eloise looked helplessly across at Jem as the first tear started to fall.

She didn't know when he moved to sit beside her. All she felt was the moment when his arms wrapped around her and held her close against the muscular strength of his body. She clutched at him helplessly, as though he were her anchor in a stormy sea.

His fingers moved to stroke her hair. Soft and rhythmic. Eloise lay still, curled within the circle of his arms. It was rather like she imagined it must feel to be washed ashore after a storm. Suddenly safe and at peace.

She knew the moment when he sensed she'd stopped crying, because his hand stilled against her hair. Then he moved, but only to settle her more comfortably in his arms, her back resting on his chest, her head laid back on his shoulder.

The small voice of caution warned that the sensible thing to do would be to move away. Instead she relaxed into the cocooning safety of being held by him.

'How are you feeling?'

Eloise had almost forgotten her cold. Had forgotten everything but the sensation of hearing the soft, regular beat of his heart. 'I'm sorry—' she began, but he interrupted swiftly.

'Don't.'

It held her silent. She knew exactly what he meant. They'd come too far together for any apology to be necessary. He knew so much of her journey…because he'd walked it with her.

A deeply compassionate, empathetic man. From the very first he'd made her feel safe. He did that now. She felt safe. Protected. Loved.

Loved. The truth imploded in her head. Laurence's words echoed in her head: 'a hundred small decisions' and then 'as important as breathing'.

· How had that happened to her? Was it really too late?

Each tiny step had been taken completely unawares— almost. Focused primarily on her father, she hadn't paid enough attention to the man standing at her side.

Jem.

She loved him.

Eloise lay against his chest, not daring to move. It was an exquisite agony. As long as she remained silent his arms would stay about her. She would have this moment.

Later he would leave and she would be alone again. It had to be that way because she couldn't cross the divide into his world. She couldn't risk the rejection.

'I haven't given you my present yet,' Jem said softly.

'You haven't?'

He shifted her slightly and leant across for his jacket. 'I nearly didn't…but when I saw it I thought of you.' He handed her a square parcel.

Reluctantly Eloise sat up and faced him. She felt so vulnerable, as though by looking into his eyes he would be able to see what she was feeling.

'It was made by a friend of mine.'

Eloise lifted the lid and stared down at an intricate twisting of platinum vine leaves shaped into a narrow bangle. 'I can't. I—' She felt as though the carpet had been pulled out from under her.

It was exquisitely beautiful—and it was from him. But it was obviously expensive. The kind of jewellery you would see specially lighted in a window in Bond Street.

'Put it on. It's nothing.'

Hundreds of pounds of nothing. Eloise let him fit the bangle around her wrist. Was this how her mum had felt? Completely intoxicated. Overcome by an emotion she'd never experienced before.

'Happy Birthday.'

'Thank you,' she said quietly. No one had ever given her anything as beautiful. No one had been able to afford to.

She twisted the bangle round her arm. It was a physical manifestation of the gulf between them. Jem had a personal fortune that ran into millions and a Viscount for a stepfather. It wasn't possible even if he wanted it to be otherwise.

Had her mum felt the same sense of hopelessness? Was she destined for the same lifelong heartbreak?

Jem pulled her back to rest against his chest. She went, unresisting. It was where she wanted to be.

The light faded around them until they sat in murky darkness. Every sense was heightened. She was aware of every shadow, the feel of his jumper, soft cashmere against her cheek. Her ear was attuned to the sound of his breath and her nose to the scent of his musky aftershave. Too scared to move in case the magical bubble was burst.

How could anything wrong feel so right? Had her mum felt that? Had that been the reason why she'd forgotten Laurence's wife, ill and dying? And Belinda, scared and lonely.

And what was Jem feeling? He said nothing. His arms were wrapped around her but he simply held her. Perhaps he felt nothing for her but sympathy.

His rich voice broke the silence. 'How are you feeling now?'

'Better. Better, much better.' She probably always would feel better when he was near.

'You probably need to get some sleep.'

'Yes.'

Jem lightly kissed the top of her head. Perhaps he thought she wouldn't feel it. 'I'd better go.'

His voice implied the opposite. Even with a cold, it would have been easy to ask him to stay.

And what then? What would become of her then?

Eloise wrapped her dressing gown more closely round her legs and sat up. 'My head does feel a bit foggy. I'll go back to bed.'

'Not a good way to spend a birthday.' Jem accepted her rebuff without question. He stood up and picked up his jacket. 'You'll be all right?'

'I'll be fine.' Eloise stood up and her hand touched her bangle. 'Thank you for my present. It's beautiful.'

He hesitated, as though he had been about to say something else. 'You're welcome.'

'Thank Laurence for me, if you speak to him. I'll telephone him, but…' She trailed off, her eyes falling before the intensity of his.

'Perhaps we could meet for lunch some time?'

She looked up. 'Some time would be good,' she said with a slight stress on the 'some time'.

'I've got to fly out to Milan tomorrow, but after that… We could have dinner.'

'That would be…great.' Except it wouldn't be. In real life Cinderella would have been miserable in her palace with Prince Charming. She wouldn't have known how his world worked. It was no different for her.

But if he really loved her?

But no, the rational part of her brain cautioned. She would always be his stepfather's illegitimate daughter— never quite good enough.

Jem reached out and pushed back the hair across her face. He smiled. 'You look totally washed up. Get some sleep.'

She nodded.

'I'll see myself out.'

CHAPTER NINE

ELOISE woke when the morning sunlight streamed through the narrow chink in the curtains. It could all have been a dream, but it wasn't. The book her father had given her lay on the wooden chest and Jem's bangle was still clasped around her arm.

She rolled over and looked at her bedside clock. She'd slept for over twelve hours. She couldn't believe it. For the first time in days her throat didn't feel lacerated and her head had cleared. She might not feel like she could climb Mount Everest, but she did at least feel as though she might live.

Eloise got out of bed and went to the kitchen. She turned her nose up at her usual muesli and settled for some hot buttered toast and a cup of tea.

Jem was in Milan. Or about to go to Milan. She remembered that much from the day before. And she'd agreed to have lunch with him. Or dinner? Either way she'd taken another small step in a direction she wasn't at all sure she wanted to go.

Actually, that wasn't true. She did know she wanted to be with Jem. It was almost like an addiction. He filled her mind completely. It would be easy to pretend the outside world didn't exist. For a time.

And there was the problem. It could only be for a time. Laurence and her mum had discovered that. Real life would always be there, just brushing at the edge of their consciousness. So what was the point of beginning something that could have no future?

She felt as if she was a tiny fish hooked on a line. Slowly but surely she was being reeled in—and there was nothing she could do about it.

All her protestations were as effective as a little fish thrashing about. Totally futile. The end result would be exactly the same. She was going to get hurt.

She knew it with the same certainty she knew her name. He might look at her as though she kept his world turning, but that didn't mean he loved her.

Not as she loved him. Eloise curled up at the end of her sofa and picked up a pile of her mother's papers. She'd not wanted to fall in love.

But with Jem that had all changed. She knew exactly how her mum had felt, all those years before. It was destiny. Some alignment of the stars had predetermined this would happen. There was nothing she could do but give in to the wave of emotion that was Jem.

Her fingers flicked through the top few sheets on the first pile. *How could one person have generated so much paperwork?* Her mum had even made lists of jobs she had to do. There was a sheet costing out a four-day break to Barcelona. Eloise hadn't known her mum had even wanted to visit Barcelona.

In all her forty years her mum hadn't parted with anything. She'd kept her own school reports, her swimming badges and her RSA III typing certificate, passed with a distinction. It was going to be difficult to discard any of them. No wonder she hadn't been able to face sorting it all out six years earlier.

Further into the box Eloise found piles of letters. Correspondence from long ago, all sorted with meticulous care and held together with elastic bands.

Her grandma's handwriting, immediately recognisable,

was on the envelopes of the first pile. The date stamps showed they'd been posted while her mum had been pregnant with her. Eloise laid her letters to one side. She didn't want to read about her grandma's disappointment.

The next pile was in a hand she didn't recognise. Eloise slipped off the elastic band and opened the first letter. It had been written a little earlier, during her mum's stay at Coldwaltham Abbey, and was from a girl called Janice.

A friend?

She couldn't place anyone called Janice. Presumably their friendship had died a natural death. Perhaps when her mum had decided to stay in Birmingham and keep her baby?

The letters were light and chatty. Full of the kind of details that would interest a girl of nineteen. There was a description of a party and a new dress.

Eloise took a sip of tea and picked up the next letter in the pile. No mention at all of Laurence, so she could only assume her mum had kept her own counsel. Probably wise. Janice had met a mechanic called Steve and they were going to the cinema.

The letters were addictive. Like reading someone's diary. You knew you shouldn't, but…

Eloise read on through the pile. Her hand hesitated on a letter where the address changed. Her mum had moved to Birmingham.

Which meant her mum had discovered she was pregnant. Eloise pulled out the thin sheet of paper. Janice's tone had changed. Her writing was more stilted, as though she hadn't been sure what to write.

And then Eloise read a line that tore the bottom out of

her world and sent her into free fall. A single line, but it had the destructive power of a napalm bomb.

You must know who the father of your baby is.

The words didn't seem to make sense. Eloise ripped open the next letter. Her mum's side of the conversation was missing. She read a stream of dates as Janice tried to work out who had been where and when. And then there was Patrick McMahon. A sailor whom no one knew how to trace.

Oh God, no. She felt the blood drain from her face and her body become icily cold as she understood what she was reading.

Her mum had left Coldwaltham Abbey on the nineteenth and she had met Patrick on the twenty-second. *Was that possible?* Had her mum really taken two lovers in the middle of her monthly cycle? Was it really possible she hadn't *known* who the father of her child was?

It was clear from Janice's words that she'd known who she *wanted* to be her baby's father. Perhaps that was why she'd never told her daughter who her father was? And why she'd not made contact with Laurence after his wife had died?

It might even explain the letter she'd left with her will. In the natural course of things Laurence should have predeceased her. Maybe she'd thought it would be safe to tell her daughter about the father she hoped she had.

Thoughts, questions, memories all flitted through her head like an old time slide show.

And then Eloise realised just how much she'd lost. How much it had mattered to her that she had a father. It had been so important to know *who* she was. That her father was the 'good man' her mum had described. To feel she had a place in the world and know what that place was.

Now she'd been cast adrift. She belonged nowhere. She didn't know who she was. Or who her father was—possibly Laurence, possibly not.

As the initial shock passed she felt the pain. It felt as if acid was running through her veins. Every new thought brought a fresh realisation—and then the one that brought the tears coursing down her face.

Laurence. Somehow she'd come to love him like a father. She *wanted* him to be her father as much as her mum had obviously done. It felt as if she was being torn from the family she so desperately wanted to belong to.

Until this moment she hadn't known she'd felt like that. She'd thought it was all still in her control. In reality it wasn't like that. As Laurence had opened up the inner sanctum of his family she'd slipped inside. She couldn't explain how it felt to know she was going to have to stand back on the outside. To have no half-sister. No half-brother.

To have no one.

Eloise sat in stunned silence, her tea cold beside her and her face streaming with tears. She'd thought she knew all about loss, knew every possible ramification it brought.

But this…

This was beyond anything she'd ever experienced. This was the kind of blow you would never recover from and it hadn't run its course yet.

She had to tell Laurence. She couldn't let him go on thinking he had a second daughter when it was quite possible he didn't. She had to ring him and thank him for her present and tell him…

Dear God, she couldn't do it. But there was no alternative. To hide this new knowledge would be wrong. *Her mum hadn't known for sure.* She had to tell him.

Did Laurence know anything about Patrick McMahon? Somehow Eloise doubted it. Patrick had happened after Nessa had left Coldwaltham. After she and Laurence had decided they couldn't continue with their affair.

Had her mum been so distraught she'd stumbled into another man's bed? Eloise didn't dare to make any assumptions. She couldn't know.

Eloise stood up shakily and stuffed the letters into her handbag. She mustn't give herself time to think. She had to act now. Quickly. She had to get down to Sussex immediately. She had to tell Laurence face to face.

Eloise looked every inch the professional. Her hair had been swept up into a neat chignon and her make-up was flawless. Inside she might feel like she was dying but outwardly everything was as it should be.

'Gullivers supplied the tiara for Lilly Bamber's wedding to that rock star. What was his name?' Cassie asked, drawing on a cigarette.

'Garth Ryman.'

'That's it! Can't stand his music.' She stubbed out her cigarette on the pavement. 'I wish smoking wasn't banned inside. Are you coming?'

Eloise nodded. This was business. Work. Somehow she'd managed to go through the motions for the past two weeks.

'Every diamond in the tiara was flawless. Must have been worth thousands. Personally I don't know how you tell. Still, everyone who's anyone should be here…which is all excellent fodder for the magazine.'

Which was all that mattered, Eloise reminded herself as she followed in her boss's wake. The magazine. Her career. Her future.

Cassie was right. Anyone who was anyone had made a beeline for Gullivers tonight. The paparazzi were out in force and there were easy pickings.

Caleb, the photographer *Image* had sent to cover the opening of Gullivers' flagship store, seemed more than happy. She watched as he snapped a cruel shot of some society hanger-on.

Same people, same venues. Almost. Last month it had been a new fashion store, but the feel was the same. It was all faintly ridiculous. Eloise walked along the red carpet and avoided the mini-skirted girl who had been hired to sprinkle rose petals.

It was then that she saw him.

Jem.

Back from Milan. She'd missed him. She hadn't realised how much until she saw him.

His face was turned away for the moment, and then he spun round. His blue eyes sought her out as though they were programmed to find her among the heaving throng.

She'd wondered how she'd feel when she saw him again. Now she knew. Suddenly the world was a brighter place simply because he was in it. She'd expected the evening to be dull, and suddenly it wasn't.

He looked amazing. For someone who professed to dislike society life so much he managed to fit in effortlessly. Which, of course, he did. He'd been born to this.

Whereas she'd clawed her way into this life. Her white trouser suit was borrowed and would be returned in the morning. The long diamond earrings that brushed her shoulders would be returned before she left Gullivers.

She belonged nowhere.

'Hello.' His blue eyes glinted shamelessly down at her.

'Hello,' Eloise echoed foolishly, her heart pounding painfully against her ribcage. Her eyes took in the trendy stubble on his chin, the threads of grey buried deep in his black hair.

She had so much to tell him. About her discovery of the letters. About Laurence. About her abortive attempt to find out information about Patrick McMahon. So much. And yet the words she needed didn't come.

It was enough that he was here. There would be time to explain everything. Talk through all the emotions of that long conversation with Laurence. Perhaps Jem already knew.

Jem leant forward to kiss her cheek. It was the kind of kiss complete strangers were sharing all around the room, but Eloise felt as though she'd been struck by lightning.

She loved him.

And she suddenly realised she wouldn't change that even if she could. Knowing him and loving him was worth the risk.

Perhaps that was what her mum had thought. Her mum's relationship with Laurence had caught fire and crashed spectacularly, and her mum had paid a high price—but that didn't mean her fate would be the same.

Her mum had made a poor choice and there'd been consequences to that. If she'd chosen differently she could have contacted Laurence when his wife died, just a few months after she'd left Coldwaltham Abbey. Maybe, just maybe, her life would have been completely different.

'I need to talk to you,' Jem said.

'I know.' There was so much to say. It would be painful to express her feelings about her mum, but it was necessary.

Belinda passed across her peripheral vision. Eloise turned to look at the woman who might possibly not be

her half-sister after all. Laurence was right; in so many
ways it didn't matter. There would always be a bond
between them.

Belinda looked incredible. Her hair was newly cut in
a skull-hugging modern style and her clothes were cutting
edge. She was barely recognisable from the woman she'd
been when Eloise had first met her.

Jem let out a slow whistle. 'You look marvellous.'

She reached out and held Eloise's hand. 'I had help.
This woman's a genius.'

'An easy project. Belinda's got a bone structure mod-
els would kill for.'

'And the clinic?' Jem asked.

Belinda again glanced at Eloise. 'One day at a time,
one day after the other.' She smiled, a new confidence in
her face. 'I'm an out-patient.'

'And Piers?'

A slight shadow passed over her face. 'Is with Corinne
Risborough.' She held up a hand to stop the comment
forming on his lips. 'I've always known; it's just time I
stopped pretending.'

Jem cast an amazed glance across at Eloise.

'You must have known it,' Belinda said, smiling
bravely. 'I think everyone knew. He wasn't very dis-
creet.' She waved a hand at a woman at the far side of
the shop. 'I'll see you both later. I've just seen someone
I know.'

'I couldn't believe it when Laurence told me,' Jem
said, watching his step-sister thread her way across the
room.

'She's done really well.'

Jem turned back to look at her and Eloise held her
breath, waiting for what he'd say next.

So much rested on what he said. Did he blame her for

not checking her mum's paperwork thoroughly before contacting Laurence? She blamed herself, although she couldn't regret the outcome.

Nevertheless, she had to admit she'd caused a great deal of pain and soul-searching.

Cassie had told her not to be so foolish when she'd finally confided in her. Her worldly counsel had been a soothing balm, but she needed to hear from Jem.

It was still a fact that Laurence and her mum had been lovers. It was still possible that she was his daughter…

'You're Eloise Lawton,' a female voice said at her elbow.

Eloise pulled her gaze away from Jem and looked down at…Sophia Westbrooke. It took no more than a moment to identify the petite blonde, even though she'd only seen her at a distance.

The teenager's outfit was as expensive as before. If she judged it correctly, it was another Yusef Atta creation. The peacock embroidered on her kaftan-style top showed all the hallmarks of his exquisite work.

This time she'd teamed it with a pair of well-cut jeans. It was an effortlessly stylish creation and she wouldn't have had change out of a couple of thousand pounds.

'Yes, I am.'

'I thought you must be. I love your column.' Sophy tucked her arm inside Jem's, glancing up at him. 'I was wondering where you'd got to, darling,' she said in a voice that was surprisingly husky.

The familiarity in her voice and the way she threaded her fingers through his made Eloise feel as if a branding iron had been pushed into her heart.

Sophia Westbrooke had the right kind of pedigree. She was *exactly* the kind of woman someone of Jem Norland's background required. She was young, beautiful, malleable and clearly adored Jem. What more could he want?

It wouldn't be someone like her. Only in fairy tales did the stepson of a Viscount fall in love with a member of the proletariat. For a moment she'd allowed herself to forget that.

Blithely unaware of how Eloise was feeling, Sophia turned back to her. 'I buy *Image* all the time. This is a Yusef Atta,' she said, holding out the hem of her floaty top.

Eloise knew she said everything that was appropriate. She somehow shifted into professional mode and Eloise, the ambitious career girl, took over.

Sophia Westbrooke's father was the principle shareholder of Westbrooke and Dyer. She could almost hear Cassie's hissed instructions as though her boss had been by her side to say them. *Worth millions, darling. The Westbrookes know everyone. Tread carefully.*

Eloise, consummate professional, smiled. 'I'd better circulate. I hope you both have a lovely evening.'

She made it as far as the door before Jem caught up with her. 'Where are you going?'

'Out.'

'Why?'

Eloise looked up at him speechlessly. He probably didn't know. He'd been living in his ivory tower so long he probably didn't know that other people lived by different standards, a different moral code. He might have kissed her, but it probably meant nothing to him.

'Go back to Sophia.'

'Sophy is Andrew's girlfriend,' he said, catching her arm. 'Lord Andrew Harlington. He's a friend of mine.'

'He is?'

Jem's smile slowly twisted and his eyes lit with sinful laughter. 'You thought Sophy and I...'

'It's possible,' Eloise said stiffly.

'It isn't,' he shot back. 'I kissed you. What did you think that was about?'

'Men do that, particularly from your class.'

'Class, my...' He stopped just in time. 'That's the most arrant piece of inverted snobbery I've heard in my entire life.'

Eloise looked down at her white trousers, feeling strangely ashamed. Jem reached out and lifted up her face to look at him. 'Interesting, though.'

'Is it?'

'Despite what you may have heard, the days of catching the parlour maid unawares have long gone.'

The laughter in his voice brought a pinkish colour to her usually pale cheeks. She looked self-consciously over one shoulder.

Jem moved his thumb across her cheek. 'We'll develop this later.'

Eloise risked a shy glance up at him. 'I'd better circulate.'

He stepped back. 'Just don't try and escape without me.'

She wouldn't do that. Eloise watched him thread his way back into the throng. Her stomach was churning with nervous excitement...and happiness. She was almost daring to believe the dream. That maybe, just maybe, it was possible.

Eloise passed the next half an hour with a glorious sense of optimism. She felt like a rosebud slowly unfurling in the hot sun of a summer's day.

She earned Cassie's approval by managing to talk for

at least ten minutes to the current face of Lancôme. It was all going so well.

And then she saw Piers Atherton. It had been a kind of sixth sense that made her look up at exactly the right moment to see him slither into Gullivers, a stunning-looking woman hanging off his arm.

Eloise instinctively sought out Belinda. She saw an expression of acute misery pass over her face as she immediately made excuses to the man she was talking to. Suppressing the desire to tell Piers exactly what she thought of him bringing Corinne to a place he knew his wife would be, she quickly negotiated a way through the small chatting groups.

Belinda had stood still for a moment and then gulped as though she'd been slapped. Eloise watched helplessly as the other woman headed for the exit.

Her instinct was to follow, but she had several thousand pounds worth of Gulliver diamonds hanging from her ears. It took a minute or two to find a security guard, unclip them and sign the appropriate forms. A few more seconds to hand Cassie her handbag for safe-keeping. Only then was she free to follow Belinda out into the night.

There were groups of people all round the entrance, some sipping champagne, others having followed Cassie's example and popped out for a cigarette break. The petal-strewing nymphet had long gone.

Eloise looked up and down the pavement, deciding finally to turn left as it was the quickest way to the tube station. It seemed improbable that Belinda would head for public transport, but where else had she gone?

She made a couple of tentative enquiries but no one had noticed her pass. There was no sign of her at all. Eloise headed back to Gullivers.

It was the merest chance that made her look up a side alley. She recognised Belinda's dress before she saw what was happening to her. Three youths, two male and one female, were standing around her. All wore tracksuit tops and had the hoods pulled up around their heads.

'Belinda,' she began, breaking into a run as she saw one youth push his victim hard against the wall. 'Belinda,' she said again more loudly. 'Help. Someone.'

It was the impulse of a moment. A mixture of anger and friendship, certainly a need to protect. Eloise didn't think of the danger or the possible consequences to herself.

She only thought of Belinda. How far she'd come in such a short time and how frightened she must be now.

'Help,' Eloise shouted again, as two of the attackers ran off in the opposite direction. The other sprinted towards her.

As he passed he grabbed at her shoulders and thrust her hard against the wall. His hand went for the platinum bangle on her wrist.

It all clicked in her head. All the evenings she'd spent at her self-defence class. Everything she'd learnt to try and rid herself of that insidious feeling of vulnerability.

Her tutor's words echoed in her ears. *'The only wrong move is no move at all.'*

He pushed her face up against the rough surface of the brickwork as he struggled to remove her bangle.

'No,' she shouted with an energy that was rooted deep within her. At the same time she rammed down with her heel.

She heard his yelp of pain, followed by a string of swear words, many she'd never heard used in that particular combination before.

And then she was free. He took off in the direction of

the main road. Eloise spared the merest second to look after him before she ran over to where Belinda was slumped on the ground.

She had a nasty cut under one eye and her lip was already swollen.

'Belinda?' Eloise knelt down beside her, heedless of her white suit.

Slowly the tears began to fall down Belinda's battered face. She looked up at Eloise with a pitiful, 'You were so brave. Why can't I do that?'

'Nonsense. Have they broken anything?'

Belinda shook her head, 'I don't think so.' She hiccuped. 'They wanted my engagement ring.'

Eloise heard the sound of voices and feet running. She twisted her head, first in alarm and then in relief as she saw Jem.

He was beside them in a moment. Jem glanced quickly across at Eloise and then concentrated on Belinda. He took in the vacant expression in her eyes, the cuts on her face. 'Can you stand?'

'I don't think so.' Her tears were falling steadily.

Shock, Eloise recognised. She stood back, but Belinda called her nearer.

'What happened?' Jem asked, looking across at Eloise.

'She was being mugged. Two of them ran away when I arrived.'

'And the other?' he asked quickly.

'Eloise kicked him.'

He looked down at Belinda and then up at Eloise. 'You were mad.'

'What did you expect me to do?'

His voice became clipped. 'Use your mobile, like everyone else.'

Eloise held out her empty hands mockingly. 'Funnily enough, I forgot to bring it with me.'

Jem reached into his pocket and brought out his own cellphone. She heard him give clear, concise instructions as to where they were. An ambulance would be here in minutes.

Now that the incident was over, Eloise felt her energy levels start to sag. For a time the adrenalin had kept her going, but now she felt the start of a reaction.

It was good that an ambulance was coming. Belinda's face had become paler and there was little doubt she had some sort of concussion.

It was also good that Jem was in charge. His steady voice kept Belinda focused on him. It reminded her of how he'd held her face when she'd had difficulty breathing.

What a terribly long time ago that now seemed. But, in reality it was only a few months.

She watched as the ambulance crew arrived, followed shortly after by the police. Belinda had drifted into semi-consciousness, so there wasn't much she could tell them.

They turned their attention to Eloise and she gave them her contact details and agreed to make a statement at the police station the following morning.

Jem came to stand at her elbow. 'You ought to go to hospital too. Be checked over.'

'I'm fine,' she said, ignoring the throbbing of the graze on her cheek.

'Eloise—'

'I'm fine,' she repeated more sharply. 'I just want to go home. You go with Belinda.'

Jem didn't answer her immediately. He flicked open his cellphone and made a short call.

One of the ambulance men, a portly man who had said

his name was John, came over. 'If you've had any sort of head injury, miss, you ought to come with us.'

Eloise shook her head, suddenly wishing that they would all go away and leave her alone. Jem came over to stand by her side.

The ambulance man looked across in a mute appeal.

'I only got pushed against the wall. It's a graze,' she said, feeling her face.

'She oughtn't be left alone. Just in case.'

'I'll stay with her,' Jem said curtly.

'What about Belinda? She shouldn't be on her own.'

Jem slipped off his jacket and placed it round her shoulders. It was only then that Eloise realised she'd started to shake.

It was another reminder of that first day. When she'd first met Jem. She'd never dreamt then how much she'd come to love him.

'My mother's in London. I've rung her and she's going to meet Belinda at the hospital.'

'Oh,' Eloise managed. There was nothing else for her to worry about.

'Do you need anything from Gullivers?'

Eloise struggled to bring her mind back into focus. 'I've got a bag. It's small. White.' She blinked, trying to remember. 'I gave it to Cassie.'

Jem placed a hand in the small of her back and led her out on to the main road. Her foot was sore where she'd rammed it down hard on her assailant.

Cassie was standing outside Gullivers, cigarette in hand. She let out a loud expletive when she saw Eloise. 'What happened to you?'

'You should see the other guy,' Eloise replied, with a brave attempt at humour.

'She went to the rescue of someone who was being

mugged,' Jem cut in on the pleasantries. 'I'm taking her home.'

'Shouldn't someone have a look at the gash on your face?' Cassie said, dropping her cigarette to the ground and stamping on it. 'It looks nasty.'

'It's just a graze.'

'You haven't seen it,' Cassie objected. 'You might be concussed.'

'I'm not, I—'

Jem cut in. 'I've said I'll stay with her. We've just come back for her bag. It's white…'

Mutely Cassie handed the clutch bag over. Eloise could see the speculation light up the other woman's grey eyes, but she was too weary to do anything about it.

And it was just possibly true.

Jem had arranged for Marie to go to the hospital so he could stay with her. A small glow of optimism settled deep inside her, its gentle warmth spreading out through her veins.

It made it possible to forget the anger and the fear she'd felt earlier. In its place she felt a calm sort of contentment. A certainty that somehow everything would work out for the best.

CHAPTER TEN

JEM had never felt such a conflicting set of emotions. There was a sense of gratitude and pride that Eloise's actions had saved Belinda from greater hurt, but there was fear at what might have happened.

His ice maiden had become a fiery tiger. Now the incident was over she'd reverted to a serene blonde beauty. Her chignon remained almost intact. It was only the graze on her face and the dirt on her trouser suit that showed any sign of what had been.

He hailed a taxi. His one aim was to get her home as quickly as possible.

'You don't have to stay. I've not got concussion.'

'I promised.'

He saw the faint tilt of her lips and he felt a sense of relief. 'What happened? How did you know Belinda was in trouble?'

Eloise glanced across. 'I saw Piers arrive. Did you see him?'

'Yes,' he answered shortly.

'I assume that was Corinne?'

He nodded.

'Anyway, I looked across at Belinda and saw her face. I couldn't let her go on her own. It was a good job I followed her.'

Part of him agreed. The other part wished she'd stayed where she was—safe. 'What made you go down that side road?'

Eloise shifted in her seat. 'Oh, that was pure luck. By

the time I'd signed off the diamonds I'd lost sight of which way she'd gone.'

Eloise had looked for Belinda. And then she'd gone into battle for her. His stepsister had been lucky.

'You could have been hurt,' Jem observed quietly.

The taxi stopped outside Eloise's flat. Jem didn't ask whether he could come in; he rather assumed he would.

There was so much unspoken between them, but if there was any chance Eloise might have sustained concussion he was going to be there. Whether she liked it or not.

Her small lounge had been restored to pristine order since his last visit. Flowers sat on a side table, obviously chosen for their sculptural quality.

Eloise kicked off her shoes and picked the left one up to study the heel. 'I've rather ruined this,' she said, holding it up with a wry smile. 'I hope I damaged his foot as well.'

'Is that what you did? Stamp on his foot?'

'Absolutely. Did you know the heel is the toughest bone of the foot? A metal-tipped stiletto was an added advantage.'

Jem took in the angry tilt of her chin, the determination on her face.

'Anyway, he let go of me.'

'I imagine he did.'

Eloise turned towards the mirror and began to remove the hairpins that held her chignon in place. 'Good job, too. You don't want to know what I'd have done next.'

She pulled her fingers through her hair and turned round, her smile triumphant. 'I'm really proud of myself. I actually remembered what I'd learnt. You never quite know how you're going to react when you're in the situation.'

No, you don't. Jem could say the same for this moment. He suddenly felt as gauche as any teenager. There was so much he wanted to say to this woman. To explain.

But he felt tongue-tied and uncertain, painfully unsure of how to begin. How to express all the feelings that were beginning to take shape inside him.

He wasn't even sure whether he entirely understood what they were. It might be love. Possibly.

Who knew exactly what that emotion was anyway? As he'd seen it modelled by his father, it had all been about control and power.

And, by his stepfather, it had been about friendship and acceptance.

Where did he fall in that spectrum? Until he was sure, it was safer to stay in neutral territory. Once he said the words they'd be said for ever.

She helped him. 'I'd better have a shower. Make yourself at home, if you're determined to stay.'

Eloise turned and padded along the narrow hallway, leaving him alone in her lounge. He drew the curtains shut and switched on the side lamps.

He could hear the sound of running water and his imagination hit overdrive as he pictured her standing beneath it.

There was nothing to do but wait for her to return. The room seemed so much clearer. Her mum's boxes had disappeared from the corner. She must have finished going through them all.

He turned at the sound of her voice, muffled from the shower. 'There's some wine in the fridge. Glasses in the cupboard.'

Jem opened the fridge and pulled out the dry white wine she had there. Glasses took more effort, but he found them. 'Do you want me to open it?'

'Corkscrew in the top drawer on the left.'

He rummaged through the contents and triumphantly pulled out a serviceable corkscrew.

'Find it?' she asked, appearing in the doorway, wrapped in a short kimono.

Her hair was wet, darker than he'd ever seen it. Her face, devoid of make-up, showed the graze livid on her cheek.

And there was nothing neutral about how he was feeling. Any control he thought he had was an illusion. He wanted her with a passion that was primeval.

She must have read the spark in his eyes because she turned away with a quick, 'I'd better get some clothes on.'

'I'll pour the wine,' he mumbled.

He was drowning, and going down for the third time.

She reappeared in a soft jersey dress which wrapped around her body. He noticed, because he couldn't help it, that it appeared to be held together by one simple bow. All it would take was one easy pull…

Jem handed her a glass.

'Thank you.'

Her eyes looked luminous above the rim of her glass. Her hair had already begun to dry to a corn-gold around the edges of her forehead.

'I feel so much better after that shower.'

'I imagine you do,' he said, following her back into the lounge. 'How is it you're such an expert on self-defence?'

'I did a course.' Eloise settled herself on the sofa. 'When I was at university.'

'Very sensible.' He sat in the opposite corner.

'I was nearly attacked once. Or perhaps I was. I don't

know how you classify these things.' She sipped her wine. 'Anyway, I had a near miss.'

Jem said nothing. He waited, letting her decide when to continue.

'I was walking home from a party.' She looked up over the rim of her glass. 'Far too late, of course. It was dark and the roads were completely deserted.

'I decided it was safe enough so I kept to the main road and started to walk back to my flat. I wasn't particularly worried when I heard someone behind me. I just kept walking.

'Then I heard the footsteps speed up. I think it was the change of pace that made me anxious. So I crossed the road.'

She looked up, her eyes full of wry laughter. It was as though she wanted to soften her tale with some sort of humour.

'I'd read the book, you know. Thought I was invincible.'

As she was speaking, Jem could picture it all in his mind's eye. What surprised him was how he was feeling. It was a surging anger that anyone could treat Eloise in this way. *His Eloise.*

His feeling of possessiveness scared him. It reminded him of so much. Played to that long held, deep-seated fear that he might be like his father.

And then he looked at·her face. He minded for *her.* It was the soft, faraway look in her brown eyes that prompted every instinct he had to keep her safe. *For her.*

He wanted what was best for her. He wanted her to have the fullest life possible and to reach her potential. He wanted her to be happy.

That wasn't about control, was it? Or ownership?

'What happened?' he prompted.

'I was lucky. We were running down the pavement, but at the point at which I knew I couldn't outdistance him a bus turned the corner.'

'A bus?'

She nodded. 'A night-time bus. They must have seen me because they slowed down and one of the passengers pulled me up. Very lucky.'

Jem reached out and took hold of her hand. He threaded his fingers through hers. They were starkly pale against the tanned skin of his own.

'Very lucky.' He looked deep into her brown eyes. So deep he could see the tiny amber flecks that fanned out around her jet-black pupils, now dilated to the size of saucers. 'You should have taken a taxi.'

'No money.' Her answer sounded breathless.

Jem would have given his last penny if it would have kept her safe. *Was that what love was?*

All his life he'd known that women were attracted to his money as much as him. Brigitte Coulthard would have married a changeling if he'd had access to the millions at Jem's disposal.

His eyes flicked to Eloise's soft full lips, he noticed the tiny tremble and finally understood. It was as though huge cogs in his brain had suddenly slotted together.

Eloise wanted *him*. Despite all the fears that held her back.

And God help him, he wanted her.

None of it mattered. Not Laurence. Not Nessa. Not Belinda. All that mattered was that he'd found a woman who could see past his money to the real him.

And, he could see the real her.

Finally, he understood why he'd wanted to show Eloise his home. He wanted to share the vision he had of the barn. Share the spectacular views.

He wanted to be able to picture her in it because by being able to do that it made it feel more like a home.

Slowly he drew her closer. There was nothing casual about this. It was what made it so frightening. If he made love to her now, he would never be free of her. It was all a question of trust.

His of her, and hers of him.

Jem looked deep into her soft brown eyes and read the fear in her own. 'Trust me,' he said softly.

And he knew he was saying it as much for himself as her.

'Trust me.'

Eloise looked up at him, her eyes desperately searching for something. Some reassurance. And then she smiled. 'I do.'

With slow deliberation she reached out and pulled his head towards hers. The feel of his lips touching hers blew his mind.

He knew the moment when he felt for that tiny bow at the side of her dress. The feel of the material beneath his fingers. The soft tug as the knot held.

He felt the small resistance within Eloise, felt the slight tension and then her surrender.

It was a moment of complete euphoria. A prize won.

And then he stopped thinking at all. His lips hungrily devoured hers. His hands moved across her body, needing to touch her.

His fingers unclipped the lacy bra and he saw the soft rosy peaks of her breasts, more beautiful than he could ever have imagined.

And finally he knew what love was. There was no risk—because this was Eloise. There was no hidden agenda. No secrets. No lies.

Just the two of them. Together.

Eloise opened her eyes and looked at the sleeping man beside her. His handsome face looked scrunched against her pillow and his hair was tousled.

He'd never looked sexier, she thought, pushing back a heavy lock of hair.

And he was hers.

Was that possible?

He'd told her to trust him, and she did. For the first time since her mother had died she really believed she could trust another person.

It all felt so new and tentative, but she'd woken with a feeling of complete peace. Of rightness. Her heart felt so full it was near bursting.

There was so much that needed to be sorted if they were going to be together: he hated London, she worked there—but none of it mattered.

He'd said to trust him and she did. She trusted him to make things right for them.

Jem opened one eye and then a slow smile spread over his face. 'You're here,' he said with a note of wonder.

She felt the answering glimmer. 'I live here.'

'Then what are you doing with a man in your bed?'

Eloise appeared to consider. 'Well, he didn't seem to want to be alone last night and I thought it would be a kindness to give him a bed.'

'I don't want to be alone any night.'

'Really?'

He reached out and pulled her naked body up against his. 'Hmm, really.'

Eloise gasped in pleasure as he pressed a kiss against the small sensitive spot at the base of her neck. His hands moved to skim across her buttocks.

'I don't generally have a vacancy,' she teased.

Jem answered with a playful pinch, his blue eyes glinting mischievously.

She squirmed against him and caught sight of the clock by the bed. 'Do you know what the time is?'

'No.'

'It's gone ten o'clock.'

He rolled over and checked. 'So it is,' and made to snuggle back down.

'We ought to check on Belinda.'

Jem groaned but said, 'I'll grab a shower.'

'Towels in the cupboard and I'll make a cup of tea.' Eloise flicked her long legs and got out of bed.

Jem found he had the most amazing view. He watched as she picked up her kimono from the chair and wrapped it round her slender body.

She looked back across her shoulder like some old-time seductress. 'Get up.'

It was difficult to make his body respond. His limbs felt heavy and his heart was completely at peace. He never wanted to leave this moment.

And then he realised he didn't have to. This moment was his for all time. And there would be other moments. A lifetime of moments.

'Are you going to ring the hospital?' Eloise asked as he appeared after his shower.

'We may as well turn up on spec. She was only admitted as a precaution, so I doubt they'll keep her in.'

Eloise nodded.

'Besides, if we're barred entrance, I'll take you for a greasy fry-up in a café I know.'

She handed him a mug of tea. 'I thought you didn't know London.'

'You'll be surprised what I know.' He winked.

She left, laughing, and Jem sat down on the sofa. It

felt like a weight had been lifted from him. His life had a purpose and meaning he hadn't thought possible.

The telephone rang on the side table and Jem glanced across at it, wondering whether he should answer it. Three rings and the answering machine clicked into action.

'Eloise, pick up. Are you there?' A silence and then, 'It's Cassie.' Another silence. 'Ring me, the minute you get in. I want to know about the sex god.'

Jem picked up his tea and sipped.

'You've got twenty-four hours to ring me before I tell the team. Oh, and,' she added after a short pause, 'what about the letters?'

Jem could almost see her drawing on a cigarette.

'Eloise? Have you told him your father's name is Patrick McMahon? Ring me.'

Cassie ended the call and Jem sat in stunned silence. He couldn't process what he'd heard. It made no sense.

No sense at all.

Eloise came into the lounge. She looked exactly the same. Like an angel. Her hair swung in a bright curtain of sunshine, her deep aubergine dress hugged every curve of her body.

'Was that the phone? I thought I heard someone speaking.'

Jem put his tea down on the table and reached out to rewind the message. His eyes never left her face as the machine replayed every word Cassie had said.

He watched the blood drain from her face, her eyes enormous in her pale face.

'Jem, I…' she began.

'It seems there's something you should have told me,' he said in a voice he hardly recognised as his own. His words grated in a hard metallic sound.

She didn't move towards him. She stood by the door, frozen in that one spot. 'I—I was going to tell you. There wasn't a right moment. It happened while you were in Milan—'

Jem couldn't bear to hear any more. He held up his hand to silence her.

He'd been played for a fool. He allowed himself one last look at the elegant visage that was Eloise Lawton, scam artist. There had to be no other explanation.

She'd almost succeeded. He'd been completely taken in by her. As had Laurence. He looked at her and felt complete revulsion.

Love and hate were so very close. He had no difficulty in deciding on which side of the equation he stood.

But it didn't stop the disappointment. Or the slow sense of disillusionment, followed by the searing pain of total betrayal.

Jem said nothing. He stood up, walked to the door…and shut it. He heard her shout his name, but he didn't pause or look back.

Eloise had never felt pain like it. Not her mum's death or the news of her parentage had been anywhere on the scale of agony she now experienced. Each of those times she thought she'd reached the lowest possible point but now she discovered there were further depths to plummet.

She was being forcibly wrenched from a place of such happiness. Torn asunder.

If it was true that the physical act of making love joined two souls together, this feeling made perfect sense. It felt as if she was being ripped in half.

She went to the window and watched Jem walk away. He didn't look back. No hesitation, just a clear determination to leave her.

She watched him turn the corner and that last tiny flicker of hope died.

He hadn't waited to listen to her explanation.

He'd told her to trust him, but at the first test he'd refused to trust her.

She walked over to the answering machine and played back Cassie's message. And then again.

It sounded so damning.

But he should have waited, listened to what she had to say.

There were no tears. She couldn't feel anything. She sat in stunned disbelief.

He'd left her. It was over.

Eloise left her own tea on the table. The two full mugs were a visual mockery. It was the only sign Jem had ever been there.

She'd survive. Of course she would. People didn't really die from a broken heart. Even her erstwhile namesake had gone on to carve a successful career as an Abbess, even if life in a nunnery hadn't been freely chosen.

Eloise pulled on her aubergine boots and let herself out of the flat. The early June air held the promise of spring. Such optimism.

She went to the police station and left a detailed statement. The graze on her cheek was photographed and she heard that two of the youths had been apprehended. They'd been caught running away on CCTV. The police sergeant said there was 'no honour among thieves' and he was confident they'd catch the third.

Eloise smiled and nodded and pledged whatever support they needed. Then she took the tube to the hospital Belinda had been taken to.

Whatever Jem said, and however he felt, she still had

a responsibility to the woman who *might* still be her sister. She had to know how she was. Whether Piers had been in contact. Whether her fragile confidence remained intact.

She made it with only fifteen minutes to spare before the end of visiting hours. The nurse at the desk indicated a private room at the end of the corridor.

Eloise pinned a smile to her face, which froze the minute she saw Jem sitting by Belinda's bed.

He looked up and a bleakness passed across his face. He stood up. 'I'm just leaving.'

'You don't—'

'It's time I was going.' Jem quickly kissed Belinda's cheek and escaped.

Eloise turned in time to see the door swing shut and then looked back at Belinda, now several interesting shades of brown and yellow.

Belinda patted the chair Jem had just vacated. 'Your wounds don't look too bad,' she observed.

'They're not.' *At least not the ones people could see.* The most painful wound was the one Belinda's stepbrother had just inflicted.

'I've been to the police station. Made a statement,' Eloise continued, with an attempt at brightness. 'They photographed my face.'

'They've been here to do mine.' Belinda nodded. 'You didn't tell him.'

Eloise looked up.

'About the letters.'

Eloise put her handbag down on the floor and played for time. 'I was going to. But you were attacked… Then, well, one thing led to another.'

'Jem didn't tell me that,' Belinda said, holding her bruised face as she started to smile.

'He wouldn't listen to me. I'm sure he thinks it's all some kind of elaborate con. But I don't understand. Just what does he think I'm going to get out of it?'

'Money,' Belinda answered succinctly.

Eloise looked at her, aghast. 'I don't want his money.'

'I know that. He does too, I think.' Belinda's fingers pleated the stiff fabric of the hospital sheet. 'Give him a chance, Eloise. He'll come round.'

She'd started shaking her head even before Belinda had finished speaking. 'It's too late.'

'Only if you let it be. You didn't know Jem when he first came to Coldwaltham. He was an obnoxious boy.'

Eloise found she was listening in spite of herself.

'Has he spoken about his father?'

'A little. He said he was a bully and a cheat.'

Belinda gave a scornful laugh. 'That's an understatement. Rupert Norland was a nasty piece of work. He would make my Piers look like Mother Teresa.

'Jem is almost unrecognisable from the boy he was when he first arrived. But,' Belinda said slowly, searching for words, 'the thing is…Jem doesn't trust easily. He was lied to too often.'

'Daddy and Marie have been amazed at the ease with which you've got under his defences. He loves a few people very deeply. You threatened them, but still he couldn't help but fall in love with you.'

Eloise shook her head in mute denial. A man who truly loved her wouldn't have left her like he had this morning.

'He loves you very deeply,' Belinda said stoutly. 'I wish there was someone who felt that way about me. It's because he loves you he's hurting so much now.'

Eloise frowned. Against her will a small glimmer of hope had started to take shape.

'But I'm still not likely to be Laurence's daughter.'

'That doesn't matter.' Belinda reached out and touched her hand. 'Daddy's right. He said if you're not his biological daughter, you should have been.'

Eloise felt the tears well up behind her eyes.

'And if you're not really my sister, you should have been. Daddy told me—' she gripped Eloise's hand in a painful grasp '—he said he'd only ever loved three women. My mother. He'd loved her until the day she died. Marie.' Her voice softened. 'And your mother. But, he told me, it was your mother he let down.'

Eloise felt the tears trickle over her face and she quickly brushed them away.

'So it doesn't matter any more. I'm sure you could have a DNA test or something. But why? It won't change anything. He loves you as a daughter. So that's what you are.'

'Th-thank you.'

Belinda released her hand. 'Give Jem a chance.'

It didn't seem likely he'd want one. 'I'd better go. Visiting time is nearly over.' Eloise picked up her handbag and headed for the door. She felt as if she'd been wrung out and fed through a mangle.

She couldn't cope with all the emotions surging through her body. Her head hurt with trying to process them all and understand how she was feeling.

The signs to the exit were clearly marked. Eloise blindly followed the arrows, not really noticing anything about her surroundings.

'Eloise?' Jem's voice. Half command, half plea.

She stopped, not daring to turn round.

'I should have listened.'

She felt the tears rise up and trickle down her face. She didn't want to turn round. She didn't want him to see them.

And she heard Belinda's voice. *'Give Jem a chance.'*

She wanted to. More than anything else in the world.

But he'd let her down. He'd failed her. Just as Laurence had failed her mum. Was that inevitable? Did loving someone always mean you were going to be hurt?

'I thought you'd been deceiving Laurence. Making him believe something was true…when it wasn't.'

Eloise closed her eyes against the pain. 'I—I haven't.'

'No.'

She heard him step closer. She could almost feel his breath on her hair.

'I'm sorry.'

Her tears continued to fall, scalding on her cheeks. Sorry wasn't enough. She couldn't do it. She couldn't make herself trust him again.

'I don't know who my father is,' she managed. 'I suppose it might not even be Patrick McMahon, whoever he might have been.'

For one moment she thought Jem was going to touch her, but he didn't. He was standing so close.

She made one desperate swipe at her face, clearing away the betraying trails of moisture. Then she stepped forward, putting some distance between them before she turned round.

'I don't even know who my mum is any more. I've lost everyone…and it isn't my fault. I—It isn't my fault.' Her voice broke, her face awash with tears she no longer cared about.

'I love you.'

His words were quiet, but very distinct.

Eloise wrapped her arms around her body, as though she could shield herself from hurt.

'I love you,' he repeated, moving closer.

She let out a sob and his arms wrapped around her. 'I'm sorry. So sorry,' he whispered against her hair.

Eloise felt his fingers stroke her hair.

'I will always love you.'

She pulled away and immediately he released her. But she'd only moved far enough away to look up into his face.

It was there in his eyes. All the love in the world. For her.

Slowly she smiled. 'I love you too. I should have told you about—'

'The first part is all I need to hear.' He reached across and cradled her head, bringing her towards him for a kiss of commitment.

He leant back and looked deep into her eyes. 'Marry me.'

Her smile widened.

Jem's own smile sprang into life and his voice became more confident. 'Marry me. Stay with me until the day I die.'

Eloise nodded. She couldn't speak; the words just wouldn't come. It didn't seem to matter because he gathered her close and held her there.

She had no idea how long they stood like that, or whether anyone passed them. She felt as if she'd passed through fire and had suddenly found safety.

It was the start of a new love story. Theirs.

EPILOGUE

ELOISE missed her mum. A girl would always need her mother on her wedding day.

She would have loved all this. An August wedding with all the trimmings. Something she'd never had for herself.

Eloise picked up her bouquet, carefully chosen to symbolise all her hopes for the future. Apple blossom which spoke of better things to come. The sprig of myrtle for love.

'Ready?' Belinda asked, elegant in a stunningly cut dress the colour of a summer sky.

Eloise nodded.

'Scared?'

'No.' There had never been anything in her life she'd been more certain of. She was going down the long staircase of Coldwaltham Abbey to meet Jem.

There was nothing to be scared of. There would never be anything to be scared of.

They'd both suffered too much in the past to ever risk losing what they'd found together. They knew how precious it was.

Laurence was waiting at the foot of the stairs, his kind face shining with father-like pride. 'I remember Marie wearing that dress,' he said, reaching up to catch her hand.

Eloise looked down at her 'something borrowed'. It had been the loveliest gesture when Jem's mother had offered the use of her dress and veil. The classical cut and princess sleeves were timeless, and she loved it.

'You look beautiful.'

'Thank you.'

'Marie is already at the church.'

Eloise felt a sudden surge of excitement which didn't leave her. A bubble of happiness that fizzed like the best champagne.

At the door of the church she paused to kiss Belinda and covered her face with the veil. Then she took her father's arm.

Whatever the truth of it, Laurence would always be her father in every way that mattered. Through the misty whiteness of her veil, she set off down the aisle.

On her side of the church sat her colleagues from *Image*. Cassie, resplendent in a dramatic hat, and no doubt still sulking because they'd refused to allow their wedding to be featured.

And at the altar there was Jem. Her heart swelled with love for him. As she drew near, he reached out and took hold of her hand.

It was a perfect day. His deep voice spoke the vows she knew he intended to keep. His strong hand pushed on the narrow platinum band they'd chosen to symbolise their love.

And then the vicar pronounced them 'husband and wife'. For ever.

To the sound of the 'Wedding March' Jem led her out into the bright August sunshine. Eloise looked up at him and smiled, complete trust in her beautiful face.

There was just a moment before their guests joined them. Jem pulled out a single flower from her bouquet. He placed it in the palm of her hand and closed her fingers round it, crushing the petals.

She looked up at him questioningly.

'It's something I read,' he said, opening her hand so she could see the bruised petals. 'It's a Danish saying.'

'Which is?'

His voice deepened. 'Love is like a precious flower. It is not enough to admire it. You must also cherish and protect it.' He brushed the petals out of her hand. 'And be prepared to devote your life to it.'

Eloise needed no more. She understood everything he was trying to tell her. The promise he was making. It was a promise her heart echoed.

His expression lightened and he pulled her close to kiss her. 'I love you, Mrs Norland.'

'I love you too,' she whispered softly, as their family and friends began to gather round them.

If you enjoyed what you just read,
then we've got an offer you can't resist!

Take 2 bestselling
love stories FREE!

Plus get a FREE surprise gift!

Clip this page and mail it to Harlequin Reader Service®

IN U.S.A.	**IN CANADA**
3010 Walden Ave.	P.O. Box 609
P.O. Box 1867	Fort Erie, Ontario
Buffalo, N.Y. 14240-1867	L2A 5X3

YES! Please send me 2 free Harlequin Romance® novels and my free surprise gift. After receiving them, if I don't wish to receive anymore, I can return the shipping statement marked cancel. If I don't cancel, I will receive 6 brand-new novels every month, before they're available in stores! In the U.S.A., bill me at the bargain price of $3.57 plus 25¢ shipping & handling per book and applicable sales tax, if any*. In Canada, bill me at the bargain price of $4.05 plus 25¢ shipping & handling per book and applicable taxes**. That's the complete price and a savings of 10% off the cover prices—what a great deal! I understand that accepting the 2 free books and gift places me under no obligation ever to buy any books. I can always return a shipment and cancel at any time. Even if I never buy another book from Harlequin, the 2 free books and gift are mine to keep forever.

186 HDN DZ72
386 HDN DZ73

Name	(PLEASE PRINT)	
Address	Apt.#	
City	State/Prov.	Zip/Postal Code

Not valid to current Harlequin Romance® subscribers.
Want to try another series? Call 1-800-873-8635
or visit www.morefreebooks.com.

* Terms and prices subject to change without notice. Sales tax applicable in N.Y.
** Canadian residents will be charged applicable provincial taxes and GST.
All orders subject to approval. Offer limited to one per household.
® are registered trademarks owned and used by the trademark owner and or its licensee.

HROM04R   ©2004 Harlequin Enterprises Limited

HARLEQUIN *Presents*

Welcome to a world filled with passion, romance and royals!

The Scorsolini Princes: Proud rulers and passionate lovers who need convenient wives!

HIS ROYAL LOVE-CHILD

by Lucy Monroe

June 2006

Danette Michaels knew that there would be no marriage or future as Principe Marcello Scorsolini's secret mistress. When she wanted more, the affair ended. Until a pregnancy test changed everything...

Other titles from this new trilogy by Lucy Monroe
THE PRINCE'S VIRGIN WIFE—May
THE SCORSOLINI MARRIAGE BARGAIN—July

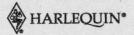
Coming Next Month

#3895 HER OUTBACK PROTECTOR Margaret Way
Men of the Outback

Sandra Kingston looks too young to be able to run the Moondai cattle station. Overseer Daniel Carson knows she will most likely need all the support he can give her. In the past Sandra has always been forced to fight her own battles, yet she can't deny that having Daniel close by her side makes her feel both protected...and desired.

#3896 THE DOCTOR'S PROPOSAL Marion Lennox
Castle at Dolphin Bay

Tragedy has left Dr. Kirsty McMahon afraid to fall in love, so when she meets commitment-phobic, gorgeous single father Dr. Jake Cameron, she assures herself that the chemistry between them will never amount to anything. But soon the attraction between them becomes too strong to ignore. Will they reconsider the rules they've made for themselves?

#3897 A WOMAN WORTH LOVING Jackie Braun
The Conlans of Trillium Island

Audra Conlan has always been fun, flamboyant and wild, until fate gives her a second chance. She will repent her mistakes, face her estranged family and evade men like photographer Seth Ridley, who's irresistible. But when her past threatens her new life, will Audra forgive the woman she once was, and embrace the woman she's meant to be...?

#3898 BLUE MOON BRIDE Renee Roszel

Roth Jerric may be drop-dead gorgeous, but he's Hannah Hudson's ex-boss, and the last person she wants around. Now they are no longer working together, and Roth can't understand why they're clashing more than usual—the tension is at breaking point. He's not looking for any romantic entanglement, but—try as he might—Hannah is one woman he can't ignore.